## "Don't you dare stand there and lie to me!"

Helen trembled as she faced her husband. "All right, I have been out with a man," she admitted. "But I have a right to go out with my friends whenever I like!"

"Oh?" Leon's voice was harsh as he continued, "And do you always dress so enticingly for your male friends? Are you trying to arouse their desire?" He paused. "Well, now I've seen you without the spinsterish disguise you always wear when you're with me—even I desire you!"

"Please don't!" Helen's eyes filled with tears as he pulled her close to his lean body. "Leon, you're not going to break your promise?"

"Why not, Helen?" he replied softly. "You are my wife."

# ANNE HAMPSON

## gates of steel

*Harlequin Books*

TORONTO • LONDON • LOS ANGELES • AMSTERDAM
SYDNEY • HAMBURG • PARIS • STOCKHOLM • ATHENS • TOKYO

published May 1973

3
73

74
976
976
77
1979

ber 1979
1980

er 1980

published in 1970

# CHAPTER ONE

THE proposition certainly sounded attractive, Helen had to admit, regarding her friend with interest. Her return fare to the beautiful island of Cyprus, plus expenses and payment for her time. All this merely for accompanying two children on the journey and delivering them safely into the care of their uncle, Leon Petrou, a Greek Cypriot living in the delightful mountain village of Lapithos, eight miles from Kyrenia on the northern coast of the island.

'It was good of you to think of me,' she said, a faint flush of eagerness erasing the sadness from her face and giving it a soft and delicate beauty. 'As you know, I haven't had a holiday for almost three years.'

'That was why I did think of you, immediately these friends of mine informed me of the position. It will be a marvellous break after your illness. November's a wonderful month for a holiday; not too hot, yet you can bathe in the sea, and sun yourself on the sands. You've mentioned a friend over there; she'll put you up for a week or two, I expect?'

'She'd welcome a visit from me.' Picking up Brenda's cup and saucer, Helen poured her more tea. 'Trudy's married to a Cypriot, I think I told you?' and when Brenda nodded, 'They have a flat just outside Nicosia; it looks lovely from the photographs she's sent me at various times.' Trudy was an old school friend, and Helen had not seen her since her marriage, six years ago, to the handsome young Tasos, whom she had met while on holiday in Cyprus the previous year. But they had corresponded regularly and several times Trudy had invited Helen to go over to the island and have a holiday with

5

them. This was a wonderful opportunity and Helen found her eagerness increasing as she asked her friend for more details.

'As I've said, it was thought at first that their father would soon be out of hospital, and these friends of mine – neighbours of his – agreed to take the children. But it's turned out that he'll be in hospital for several months, and Bill and Jean can't keep the children indefinitely. Their house is small, and they've three growing children of their own. So it's been decided that they shall go over to their uncle in Cyprus for the time being.' Brenda sipped her tea and both girls were thoughtful for a while. 'From what I can gather this uncle has most reluctantly agreed to have them, for he doesn't seem to care very much for children—' She broke off, giving a short laugh. 'Apparently he's a woman-hater, too, so he doesn't sound a very pleasant sort of person at all.'

'He certainly doesn't,' agreed Helen, frowning slightly at the idea of two young children having to live with a man like that. 'What a pity these friends of yours can't continue to have them.'

'It's impossible.' Brenda sipped her tea again and after a while Helen murmured, almost to herself,

'And he doesn't like women either.' She thought of her own attitude towards men, dwelling for a space on the reason for it. 'Has some woman done him an injury?'

'Apparently he hates women for what his brother's wife did. She just went off with someone else, leaving her husband with two babies. Chippy was two and Fiona a year younger. It was a dreadfully selfish thing to do, but some women are completely callous.'

And so were some men, reflected Helen, once again lapsing into silence as she thought of those three years with Gregory. A normally happy marriage, or so she had believed. But when her husband was found dead in his wrecked car a young girl from the office was with him.

6

'The wife is always the last to know,' a friend had said, and a great bitterness had entered into Helen as she was eventually forced to accept the fact that the affair had been going on for over a year. Well, that was the end as far as she was concerned. Her faith in men shattered for ever, she vowed never to trust one again, much less give one the opportunity of inflicting such misery on her a second time. The shock had brought on a long and serious illness which had not only drained her physically, but had impoverished her financially. After two years her health improved and she now had hopes of obtaining a post in the office in which she had worked before her marriage. But the vacancy would not occur until after Christmas, and for that reason Helen was free to take this opportunity of a visit to Cyprus.

'How old are the children now?' she asked as the thought suddenly occurred to her.

'Chippy's eight and Fiona's seven. They're lively, mind you; you'll earn your money.'

'I shouldn't expect it for nothing,' Helen returned gravely, her blue eyes clouding as she thought of her own child. He would have been four now ... but she and Gregory had had him for less than six months. 'In any case, I like children to be lively.'

'I'm afraid these two scamps are especially lively,' warned Brenda with a grimace. 'In all probability they'll become bored long before the end of the journey. Their father was once in a crash landing and that's the reason he won't send them by air. You can return by air, of course – that is, if you're interested in this proposition?'

'I am interested,' Helen responded quickly, and then, 'I shall have to see the children's father?'

'Yes, in hospital. I'll tell Bill and he'll arrange a meeting.'

Having made a favourable impression on the father, Helen was then taken by Brenda to see the children and less than a week later, having travelled to Athens by train, they were aboard the *Knossos* heading for Cyprus.

The weather was beautiful, with a clear blue sky above and the Mediterranean more like a lake than a sea.

'Is that it?' cried Fiona, pointing across to the island of Rhodes. The sun was setting behind it and a dazzling streak of fiery light splashed the sea from the island almost to the ship.

'How can that be it?' Chippy threw a look of disparagement at his sister. 'We don't land until tomorrow morning.'

The children were standing by the rail, fascinated by the strange eastern sunset, and Helen watched them broodingly from her deck-chair a few feet away. By ten o'clock the following morning she would have said goodbye to them for ever; the thought cast an odd feeling of melancholy over her and she could not help wondering at the way the children had so quickly endeared themselves to her. And with that realization came a new anxiety about the children's future, and their relationship with this uncle of theirs who disliked both women and young people. How would they fare? Presently she managed to shake off her misgivings, chiding herself and determinedly telling herself that her own duty was merely the handing over of the children to their uncle. This task once accomplished, she was free to enjoy her holiday on the island. What eventually happened to Chippy and Fiona was no concern of hers.

'Come and look, Mrs. Stewart.' Fiona turned, smiling, and held out a hand. 'Look at the shining light on the water.'

Rising, Helen dropped her book on to the chair and walked over to the rail, taking hold of the proffered hand. It was small and warm; the fingers curled round hers and Helen felt a little catch at her heart as she realized the child could not remember ever having known a mother's love.

'Isn't it pretty?' Chippy turned now and, not to be out-done by his sister, reached for Helen's other hand. 'It looks as if the sea's on fire.'

'It's certainly very beautiful,' Helen agreed, noticing the rapid descent of the sun. Even as they looked it could be seen sinking lower and lower so that the line of fire on the sea receded away from the ship and moved closer to the island.

'It's going dark— Why is it going dark so quickly?' Fiona wanted to know, turning her face up and staring at Helen in bewilderment. As she would not have under-stood, Helen merely said that in this part of the world the sun did sink quickly and, therefore, darkness came down much more suddenly.

'We won't be able to play out in the evenings.' Fiona's face wore an expression of disappointment. 'I don't think I'll like it here.'

'Course you will,' said Chippy. 'Look how warm it is. At home it was cold so you couldn't play out anyway.'

'Chippy's right,' agreed Helen, amused at Fiona's ex-pression. 'You'll be back in your summer dresses – you can wear them all the year round.'

'All the year round?' Fiona's big brown eyes became larger than ever. 'Don't they have winter here?'

Helen shook her head, but went on to say there was a period of winter, but it was very short and, in any case, the weather was still quite warm.

They watched in silence as the sky darkened and then Fiona gave an unhappy little sigh.

'I wish you were staying with us, Mrs. Stewart. I don't like you going away and leaving us with Uncle Leon.'

'Neither do I. Uncle Leon's horrid; he won't let you do anything.'

'He makes you be quiet—'

'And if you don't be quiet he looks at you like this.' Chippy's face became so contorted that Helen could not

9

help laughing, even though all her concern for the children's happiness had returned.

'I'm quite sure he doesn't look like that.' And then Helen added curiously, 'You've seen your uncle, then?'

'Yes, he's been to see us a few times—'

'Only twice, Chippy,' his sister cut in, but Chippy shook his head.

'Three times. You don't remember the first time because you were too young.'

'I'm only a year younger than you!'

'Well, you were only a baby the first time he came – but I remember him because he told Daddy I ought to be smacked.'

'Why, what had you done?'

'I can't remember, but Daddy said that Uncle Leon didn't understand children.'

'But you understand children, Mrs. Stewart,' Fiona said, tightening her grip on Helen's hand. 'Can't you stay with us?'

'I'm afraid that isn't possible, Fiona dear.'

'Is it because you don't want to?'

'No, it isn't that. But your uncle wouldn't want me.'

'Will you stay if we ask him can you?'

Smiling at Chippy's way of putting it, Helen said she was sure his uncle had already made arrangements for someone to look after them.

'But we want you,' persisted Fiona in a coaxing voice. 'Why do you have to go back? Have you got some children of your own?'

'No, I have no children of my own.' It almost seemed as if Fiona in her childish way had sensed the sadness in Helen's tone, because her grip tightened and Helen responded with an affectionate little squeeze of her fingers. 'Look, can you see the outline of the castle?' She pointed towards the island, hoping to divert the children, but neither seemed interested. A dejection seemed to have

10

come over them as they realized how close they were to the end of the journey.

Their dejection remained with them during dinner and as she watched them Helen thought they could hardly be described as lively.

Later, in their cabin, she tried to coax them out of their melancholy, saying that, even if they were not perfectly happy with their uncle, it was only a temporary stay; they should be returning to their father in a few months' time.

'Are you going straight home when you leave us in the morning?' Chippy asked, refusing to be consoled.

'First of all I'm having a holiday with a friend of mine who lives in Cyprus,' she told him, leaning across to straighten the blanket over him. 'And then I shall be going home, to England.'

'How long are you staying here?'

'Two weeks, probably.' Her tones held a slight uncertainty, for although she had cabled Trudy informing her that she was coming, she had not received a reply. But probably it had arrived after she had left, Helen thought, hoping her visit would not inconvenience Trudy and Tasos in any way.

The island was in view when, at seven o'clock the following morning, Helen left the children sleeping and went out on deck. The horizon was cut by a streak of fire as the great ball of the sun rose from behind the rim of the world. The ship was heading due east, running along-side the south coast of the island but keeping some distance from it.

'Paphos,' someone said, and Helen turned, smiling Robert Storey was travelling alone, returning from a visit to his parents in England. He had spent much time with Helen and the children, sharing their table for meals and sitting with them on deck. They'd had it practically to themselves, for only a mere handful of the people were making the voyage, November being the slackest month of the whole year. 'It will be three hours or so before we dock.'

'So long?' Helen glanced across to the island again, surprise in her voice. 'It looks so close.'

'It's quite a distance from Paphos to Limassol. Paphos, as you can see, is right over at the western side of the island.' He moved closer to Helen, but she did not edge away. Even though she had not much time for men she could not help liking Robert, with his clear blue eyes and open expression. He was a bachelor, he had told her, and after having spent a long holiday on the island, he had grown so much to love it that he had bought a tiny cottage on the hillside and cleverly converted it. He was an artist and, strangely, he lived in Lapithos. He knew Leon Petrou, but only by sight.

'He's a formidable character,' Robert had told her when she mentioned the reason for her being here. 'Confirmed bachelor – but of course he will have his – er – diversions.'

Helen had blushed at that, but Robert only laughed, and added to her embarrassment by going on to say that no Cypriot could live without a woman.

'They will openly tell you this. The climate is their excuse – or perhaps "explanation" is a better word, for the Cypriot would never dream of excusing his conduct.'

'What is his house like?' Helen had asked curiously, hoping to get some sort of picture of the home to which the children would be going.

'Ah . . . that is something,' Robert replied, his tones revealing his admiration. 'It's built on stilts in the foothills of the mountain – a great white bungalow with balconies to every room. The view from the back is of the Kyrenia Range and from the front you have the coastal plain, with orange and lemon trees – oh, and a dozen

12

other sorts – and then the great expanse of blue sea. From the side balconies you have the panoramic view of both mountains and sea. It's very beautiful indeed; far too romantic and fairy-tale-like for a crusty old bachelor like Leon Petrou.'

'Old? I thought he was quite young.'

Robert shrugged and said uncertainly,

'He's probably in his late thirties – and very handsome, I might add. But there's an air of arrogance about him that, as I've said, gives him a rather grim and formidable appearance.'

'I hope the children will be all right with him,' Helen had murmured, feeling quite sure they could not possibly be all right with him.

'I don't know,' was the doubtful rejoinder. 'It surprises me that he'd take them, for it's said in the village that patience and understanding are definitely not his virtues. I expect all hard-headed business men are rather like that. Money seems to be their only concern in life.'

'What does he do?'

'Well, for one thing he owns several packing-sheds in Famagusta – that's where all the fruit from that area is packed and made ready for export. Then he deals in land – owns much land himself in various parts of the island. And anyone who owns land here these days is likely to become a millionaire overnight.'

Robert had supplied a few more details about the children's uncle, and as he proceeded Helen found herself becoming more and more uneasy. The children had suffered enough already without being made unhappy by the severe and restrictive attitude of this uncle who, it seemed certain, did not relish the idea of having them in his home. But there was nothing she could do about it and once again Helen chided herself and determinedly erased the matter from her mind.

'Just look at that sun, and that sky,' Robert was saying,

bringing Helen out of her reverie. 'It's a wonderful island; such a pity you're not going to live here.' He paused and turned. 'But you're staying a couple of weeks, you say? Can I take you around some time?'

'I shall be with my friends,' Helen smiled. 'But thank you all the same.' She did not want his company – or any man's company – but she could not tell him that. 'I shall be based in Nicosia, in any case. I expect we shall go around from there – if my friend and her husband have the time to take me, that is.'

Again Robert shrugged, but went on to say he would give her his telephone number and she must ring him if at any time she found herself at a loose end.

'Thank you,' she said again, without the least intention of taking advantage of his offer.

The effect of brilliant gold was disappearing as the sun rose higher, slanting through the wisps of cloud which floated like a silver veil across a sky of vivid blue. Its reflection on the sea brought a dramatic clarity to the light and the island seemed only a stone's throw away. There was not so much as a ripple on the sea, not the faintest sway to the ship as it continued its progress along the southern coast of the island.

'I must go and see to the children,' Helen said at last. 'They're sure to be awake by now.'

The *Knossos* docked at Limassol at ten o'clock and a car was waiting. But even before Chippy spoke Helen knew that the man approaching her was not Leon Petrou.

'This isn't Uncle Leon.'

'You're Mrs. Stewart?' The man was swarthy and short but his smile was spontaneous and friendly. He grinned down at the children and one hand fondled Fiona's dark hair. 'Mr. Petrou sent me,' he went on as Helen nodded in answer to his question. 'He can't come himself – because a client called unexpectedly at the office – and so I take you to him.'

14

Helen blinked.

'Me? Did he say I had to accompany the children? I understood I was to leave them here, at Limassol.'

At that a small hand crept into hers and she glanced down to see a look of pleading on Fiona's lovely face.

'That's what he say.' For a moment the man appeared to be uncertain. 'Do you think I make a mistake?' But he immediately shook his head. 'No, I don't make a mistake, because he say to the office girl go and telephone the hotel and reserve a table for four, for lunch.'

At that Helen felt the tenseness in Fiona's grip relax and she smiled affectionately down at her. Chippy too was looking happier and a grin actually appeared on his small and freckled face.

'Come on, then, in you get,' she said brightly as the man opened the door of the car. 'Where are we going?' She turned to the driver. 'Not to Lapithos?'

'No, to Nicosia; that is where Mr. Petrou has his office.'

This lift was opportune then, for Helen had expected to have a taxi to take her to Trudy's flat.

The office of Leon Petrou was outside the city centre. A new building, with a wide verandah, it looked more like a modern villa than an office, and Helen gave an exclamation of surprise when, after bringing the car to a standstill, the driver got out and opened the door.

'Shall I take out your luggage?' he asked Helen, although his attention was on the children, who were standing by the car looking downcast again even though Helen was still with them.

'Perhaps you will leave it in the car for a few moments?' she said. 'I shall have to get a taxi.'

'I leave the luggage in here, then, yes.'

A moment later Helen was in a sumptuous office, standing at one side of the desk, looking up at Leon Petrou who, on their entry, had risen from his seat and was now extending a hand to Helen. She reached across the desk and felt the firmness of his grasp as he said, in a clipped and quiet tone, 'Good morning, Mrs. Stewart; I trust your journey was not too harassing.' His accent was so slight as to be scarcely noticeable.

'I enjoyed it immensely, thank you, Mr. Petrou.' She did not smile as she withdrew her hand, and he stood for a moment regarding her in silence. Then his eyes strayed to the children. She had chided them, Helen recollected, saying their uncle could not be so severe as they would have her believe – but now she knew that both they, and Robert, had been right in their description of him. She noted the hardness and the rigidity of his dark features; she saw the inflexible line of his cheeks and jaw, the tautness of his mouth and the metallic quality in his eyes which seemed, as he stood there in the shadows, to be black rather than the characteristic dark brown of both the Greek and Turkish Cypriot. His hair, immaculately brushed and shining, was black but lightly sprinkled with grey at the temples. Robert had said he was handsome. That was an understatement; he was devastatingly good-looking, but, as Robert had hinted, his looks were marred by his harsh and arrogant expression. It was not difficult to believe he disliked women and children.

'I'm relieved to hear that,' he said, giving her his attention once more. 'Knowing my niece and nephew I felt sure they would cause you some trouble.' He looked at them severely as he spoke and then added, 'I must thank you for bringing them safely to me.'

Helen felt her temper rise at his first words and she said, with more sharpness than she intended,

'They gave me no trouble whatsoever, Mr. Petrou. As I said, I thoroughly enjoyed the trip out here.'

Arrogance flashed at her curt tones and to her annoyance Helen felt the colour rise in her cheeks. He was disconcerting, this man; she felt she could hate him without much effort at all.

His inquiry about the journey, and his thanks, seemed superficial, stemming merely from the need to show courtesy and good manners, and again she felt a deep anxiety about the children's life with him. So odd, she thought, that only a week ago they had been strangers to her, and in a few minutes she would be saying good-bye to them for ever. For she had no intention of accepting any offer to lunch from Leon Petrou. A week . . . it seemed impossible. But children were like that; they could endear themselves to an understanding adult in the most extraordinary way, especially children like Fiona and Chippy.

Determined to shake off the perturbation which was rapidly taking possession of her, she inquired of their uncle how she would go about hiring a taxi.

'You're not leaving immediately? I've planned to take you all to lunch.'

'Thank you, but. . . .' Fiona's small hand found hers and then Chippy's cold little hand was also placed in Helen's. She felt a lump rise in her throat. Their uncle had not yet spoken one word to them. 'I – I shall be delighted to have lunch with you,' she returned, rather to her own astonishment.

'There is also the question of payment,' he went on, acknowledging her acceptance with no more than a slight inclination of his head. 'My brother advanced money for the fares and your time, I believe?'

'Yes, that is correct.'

'But your expenses – what about those?'

'Mr. Petrou gave me some extra money.'

'Enough?'

'Yes – yes, thank you.' She had not meant to hesitate, but he had noticed it and he asked again if his brother had given her enough. His gaze was fixed on her and she found it impossible to lie. However, she merely said,

'This trip has enabled me to have a holiday here – in

Nicosia – with friends of mine. I'm quite satisfied,' she added hastily as he began to extract some notes from the wallet he had taken from his pocket.

'This is our money, naturally, but you will find it easy to understand. Our pound is equal to the English pound, and you will find that in the shops prices are often given in English money as well as in *mils*.' He was handing her the notes; Helen opened her mouth to refuse, but something in his expression stemmed the words on her lips. 'I think this will be enough to cover what expenses you have incurred on the journey.' Helen found herself accepting the money, although it was very much against her will, for she was sure she was taking far more than she had spent.

'Thank you,' she murmured, putting the money in her bag. Both children were watching her, waiting to take her hands again. Noticing their action as they did so, their uncle at last gave his full attention to them. By some miracle his stern lips actually curved in a smile!

'How did you enjoy the journey? Were you tired on the train?' His question was directed at neither in particular and it was Chippy who replied.

'We slept at night – it was fun in the bunk beds. Mine was up high. Fiona wanted to go up high, but she was frightened of the ladder.'

'I wasn't! I wanted to sleep near Mrs. Stewart, that's why I didn't go up there.'

'In the daytime – weren't you tired of the long journey?'

'Sometimes we were tired, but Mrs. Stewart told us stories. Then we played games.'

'Games?'

'Mrs. Stewart brought lots of card games and we all played those.'

'She brought some story books too, and so we could have a read.' Fiona gave her uncle a rather hesitant smile as she spoke, but he appeared not to notice. His dark eyes registered surprise as they moved to rest on Helen's face.

'You thought about things like that?'

'I knew they'd be bored, so I decided to do something about it.' He would never have made any such preparation, she thought, and so he would naturally have had trouble with the children.

'You seem most efficient, Mrs. Stewart.' A pause and then, 'You are married?' Curiosity in his tone and his eyes. He was probably concluding that she had a husband. And here a wife could not make such a journey alone.

'I'm a widow,' she said quietly, and he murmured an apology. Then he added,

'You're young to be widowed?'

A question; Helen said,

'I'm twenty-six. My husband died two years ago, in an accident.' Again Leon made an apology, then asked if she had any children. 'Our baby died at six months old,' she returned, a sudden huskiness entering her voice. Always she would wonder if, had their child lived, he would have kept Gregory by her side.

'I beg your pardon, Mrs. Stewart,' came the surprising apology, and it did seem to Helen that his voice had lost some of its hardness as he added, 'You've had a sad life for one so young.'

The children were listening with interest, and both obviously understood, for Fiona asked,

'Has your daddy died, Mrs. Stewart?'

'Yes, Fiona.'

'And your little baby?' put in Chippy, his clasp tightening round her fingers.

'Yes, my baby too—'

'Do not ask such questions.' Leon looked sternly from one child to the other. 'You should not answer them, Mrs.

Stewart.'

'It's all right,' she smiled. 'I don't mind at all.'

Leon seemed about to make some comment on that, and then changed his mind. He sent for refreshments and an hour later they were at the Hilton, having lunch. When it was over and they were outside standing by the car Leon asked Helen for the address of her friend.

'I will drive you there,' he said, scanning the paper she handed to him. 'Yes . . . this is not far from here.'

'It's good of you to take me.' Helen thanked him graciously as she settled into the seat beside him. 'Help like this makes things so much easier when one is in a strange country.'

'You would find it confusing to walk,' he admitted, 'but a taxi would have taken you right to the door.' The children chatted to Helen, but there was an underlying dejection in every word. Helen herself felt miserable and the holiday to which she had so eagerly looked forward threatened to be somewhat flat.

'This is the road. . . .' Leon had turned a corner and was now moving at a crawl, scanning the immaculate white buildings. 'It's on this side – ah, here it is.'

Helen gave a little gasp as she got out of the car. The flat was in a block of six and every window appeared to have a balcony with flowers trailing from it. In the main grounds of the building orange trees were laden with fruit and a great row of cypresses separated the block of flats from the block next to it.

'I will take my luggage.' She waited for him to open the boot, but he said she had better make sure her friends were in. 'Yes, of course.'

'Can we come with you?' asked Chippy eagerly, determined to have her until the last available moment.

'Certainly—' Helen glanced at their uncle, who to her surprise made no demur, and both children followed her up the steps to the first floor flat in which Trudy and

Tasos lived.

'You want Madame Pavlos?' A woman appeared from the next flat and asked the question as Helen prepared to ring the bell for the third time.

'Yes – do you know where she is?'

The woman eyed her for a moment and then stared at the children in turn. Helen was reminded of something Trudy had written on first coming to live in Cyprus. 'They're pets, really, but oh, do they like to concern themselves with other people's business!'

'She and her husband go to Egypt. He have to go on business. They go last Monday.'

Helen's heart sank.

'Do you know when they'll be back?'

The woman shook her head sadly.

'They go for two months. You come a long way to see them?'

'Yes – yes, I've come from England.' Bitter disappointment flooded over her. She had come all this way and she was not to see Trudy after all. She tried to smile at the woman as she thanked her and turned away. The woman continued to ply her with questions even as she descended the steps, but at last Helen and the children were back at the car.

'Mrs. Stewart's friend has gone away,' Chippy informed his uncle.

'And she won't be back for two months,' Fiona put in. Helen glanced down. The children were delighted!

'Can she stay with us until her friend comes back?' asked Chippy eagerly.

'No, Chippy, I can't stay here two months,' Helen began. She looked unhappily up at Leon. 'If you would take me to a hotel I'd be most grateful—'

'Indeed I will not,' he refused firmly. 'You will stay at my house—'

'Oh, but – no! I can't inconvenience you like that.'

A faint smile touched the hard line of his mouth as he said quietly,

'You have not heard of the Cypriot hospitality, Mrs. Stewart. You've done my brother a great favour and it will not suit me to leave you in a hotel alone.' He was holding open the car door. 'We will have to go back to the office, I'm afraid, but I can finish my business in an hour. Then I will take you to my home in Lapithos.'

# CHAPTER TWO

By three o'clock they were on their way. Happy at the unexpected turn of events, the children chatted incessantly until, eventually, their uncle told them sternly to be quiet. They ceased at once, but, twisting round to see their reaction, Helen caught Fiona pulling out her tongue at Leon's back. She frowned, but Fiona merely grinned.

'I'm afraid we've missed the convoy,' Leon was saying, as they passed through the northern outskirts of Nicosia, 'so our journey will take over an hour.' The Turks were in control of the short route across the mountains and only foreigners were allowed through unescorted. All Greeks must either join the United Nations convoy, or use the longer route. This obviously caused great inconvenience to the Greeks, but Leon spoke without any sign of animosity and Helen was later to learn, much to her astonishment, that Leon Petrou was only one of many Greeks on the island who were in fact pro-Turkish.

There was silence in the car for some time and Helen sat back, feeling strangely relaxed as she gazed at the scene through which they were passing. The region was attractive, with gleaming white villas and flats. Few gardens were without their fruit trees, still heavily-laden with oranges, lemons and mandarins. Tall palms swayed against a sky of vivid blue and everywhere there was a riot of colour as hibiscus and jacarandas and roses bloomed in profusion.

On first learning that Trudy and Tasos were away Helen's reaction was to return to England by the first available plane, but Leon had said she could stay at his home for as long as she liked, and she suddenly decided to take advantage of his offer and remain on the island for two weeks, as she had originally intended. She could then visit the places of interest – and if Leon would let her take the children she felt her stay would prove to be most enjoyable after all.

Soon they were leaving the city behind, and gradually the lush vegetation of cypress and eucalyptus and date palm were giving way to bare and arid land. Great tracts of boulder-strewn earth stretched away on all sides, brown and baked under the sun blazing down from an almost cloudless sky. Only over the mountains was there cloud; the high, fair-weather cumulus. Now and then a heavily-laden donkey would pass, its owner ambling along by its side; there was no sign of habitation and Helen was mystified as to their destination. But at times a settlement did appear, straggling up the hillside, the mud huts contrasting oddly with modern white bungalows that had obviously been recently erected. Often the bare brown earth was tilled, and already sown with grain which would appear with miraculous suddenness once the rains had come to the island.

'We begin to pass through the mountains now,' Leon supplied as the road began to wind. 'The scenery here is most dramatic.'

It was breathtaking; with every bend in the road a new vista appeared. A vista of wild heights, sometimes clothed, sometimes naked. And then suddenly, right in front, was the sea, and soon they were running parallel to it. Nothing to mar the coastline; not a house or any other building along the whole of the sea front. In a half circle rose the massive peaks of the Kyrenia mountains with here and there a tiny village nestling among the trees.

'This is Kyrenia – but you will know that. My home is eight miles from here.'

Leon Petrou's house was exactly as Robert had described it, but Helen gasped when, having at last arrived there, she stood by the car surveying her surroundings.

The mountains behind, the great expanse of blue sea in front. Was ever a house built with such a view? The children were exclaiming excitedly and Fiona said, with a hint of disbelief,

'Can you pick those oranges?'

'Certainly you can pick them.' Reaching up, he broke off a small branch and gave it to Fiona. Three oranges hung from it, complete with leaves.

His action surprised Helen, and it seemed to surprise the children too. Perhaps, thought Helen, he was not quite so formidable as she had been led to believe.

Much later, as she was changing in preparation for the evening meal, Helen dwelt for a while on the people she had met, the people who made up Leon's household. There was his sister, Koula, highly-educated and engaged to be married at the end of January. She was twenty-two and worked in an office in Nicosia. Her fiancé, Theodore – whom everyone called Teddy – was four years older and also worked in Nicosia. Helen had not yet met him, but Koula had proudly shown her his photograph. He was dark and good-looking, and Koula was plainly very much in love with him.

'I've been led to believe that most Cypriots marry for convenience,' Helen couldn't help saying on noticing the sparkle in Koula's beautiful brown eyes. 'But obviously yours is a love match.'

'Yes.' A flush spread and then Koula became serious as her smile faded. 'Eighty per cent of Cypriot marriages are for convenience,' she owned matter-of-factly. 'Not many couples fall in love.' She paused for a while and then added, 'If my brother ever marries it will be for convenience, for he is not the type of man to fall in love.' Her low and husky voice held a hint of regret. It was easy to see that she had a deep affection for Leon, although his feelings for her were not so apparent. He had been cool and almost abrupt on introducing her to Helen.

The next members of the household to whom Helen had been introduced were Asmena, Leon's aunt, and her husband, Vasilios. Asmena was most interested in Helen, plying her with questions about her life and her home in England but Vasilios merely gazed stolidly at her and played with his worry beads – in fact, the only impression which Helen had of him was the continual clicking of these beads. Were I married to him, she thought, I'd be driven mad. She wondered if Leon played with worry beads, and for some quite incomprehensible reason she hoped he didn't.

Leon's mother, stout and lined and looking much older than her sixty years, was here only on a visit. She lived in Paphos with a married daughter, but came up twice a year to see her son and Koula.

'I had to leave Mother and come to Leon,' Koula explained, 'because my work is in Nicosia. I could not have travelled to the capital from Paphos every day.'

Helen later learned that Asmena and Vasilios were staying with Leon only until January. They were having a house built, and although they had known it would not be ready yet awhile they had sold their old house, having had an extremely good offer for it.

So by the end of January, mused Helen, Leon would be alone with the children – except for the servants, that was.

The tinkling of a bell somewhere downstairs brought Helen's attention back to her toilet. Leon had said she would hear the bell ten minutes before the meal was served. She had taken a shower and was in fact almost ready. But what dress should she wear? Not that it mattered, for she had nothing really attractive. Since her determination not to look at a man again she had deliberately refrained from wearing anything that would enhance her beauty. The dress she now chose was severe and in a shade of grey that gave a sallowness to her skin and seemed to dull the blue of her eyes. Her long fair hair was drawn back unflatteringly from her face and fastened with a black ribbon. No hint of make-up on her cheeks, no lipstick to accentuate the tender curve of her mouth.

How different from Koula. She was in a dress of flowered cotton; on one wrist was a jewelled bracelet and on the other a pretty cocktail watch, her fiancé's gift to her on their engagement. She looked adorable. Love did that to you, thought Helen, her mouth curving bitterly as she recalled the idyllic period of her own engagement.

A place had been laid for her on Leon's right; the children sat opposite, both looking rather timid but managing to smile as Helen sat down. With typical Cypriot courtesy Leon had held out the chair for her and now she was being offered soup. It was in a massive bowl, and as Helen was unsure about liking it she took only a very small helping. The ladle was taken from her hand.

'You'll like it,' asserted Leon, reading her thoughts. He proceeded to increase her helping and with growing dismay she wondered how she would ever get through it. But she did and, as Leon had said, she liked it. But both children refused it. Made from goat's milk, it did have a faintly sour flavour and Helen could understand the children's aversion to it. But their uncle insisted on their trying again. Only when Chippy began to heave did he allow him to put down his spoon. Despite the child's discomfiture Helen had to smile. Leon's brother had said he had no understanding of children, and how right he was, for the first thing to know about children was that they should never be forced to eat.

The table was laden with food, and Helen herself had to be very firm, otherwise she would have been feeling rather like Chippy. Never had she seen such amounts of food put away in one meal – though she did notice that Leon himself ate sparingly. The dish of fruit was eventually passed round – oranges and mandarins, dates and figs, and even bananas – all from Leon's own garden.

'They're not figs,' Fiona said as her uncle told her to try one. 'Figs are brown.'

'My figs are green,' Leon said, taking one and putting it on Fiona's plate. 'Chippy, what do you want?'

'N-nothing—'

'Take an orange.'

'Please, Uncle Leon . . .' Chippy began to look green.

'Take one!'

'I wouldn't press him,' Helen couldn't help putting in. 'He'll be – be—'

'Very well.' But the words were snapped out; Helen knew instinctively that he was not pleased with her interference. She glanced at him apologetically, remembering she was a guest in his house.

'I'm sorry, but he really has had enough, Mr. Petrou. Young children don't take easily to a change in their diet.'

'Don't they eat oranges at home?' interposed Koula in some surprise.

'Of course – but it was the other food. We don't have oil, for one thing.'

'And we don't have those little bits of meat on a stick,' said Fiona, adding bluntly, 'They taste like smoke.'

'You've never tasted smoke.' Chippy's natural colour was slowly returning to his freckled face.

'I don't care, they still taste like smoke.'

'They're cooked over a charcoal stove,' Asmena explained, smiling at Fiona. 'We like this meat to taste like smoke.'

'I don't like the food here.' Fiona looked across at her uncle. 'Tomorrow can I have egg and chips?'

'You'll have what we have,' was the curt rejoinder. 'Very soon you'll be used to it.' Taking up a knife, Leon began peeling an apple. Fiona's eyes had sparkled at his words and for one horrified moment Helen thought she would pull her tongue out at him again, but to her great relief the child suddenly realized she would be seen by the others at the table.

When the meal was over they left the room and then took coffee on the verandah. They were served tiny cups, of the Turkish variety, and one taste was enough for Fiona.

'Ugh!' she exclaimed. Her cup was put down too hastily; the thick black liquid splashed on to the beautifully embroidered cloth, and Leon fairly glowered at his niece.

'It's time you were both in bed,' he snapped, then looked at Helen. 'Would you mind seeing to them, Mrs. Stewart? Araté will look after them eventually, but perhaps while you're here you would do it?' Araté was the servant who had just served them with coffee; she appeared dour, and Helen's heart sank at the idea of her being in charge of the children. A deep sigh escaped her as she realized that she could do absolutely nothing about it.

'Yes, certainly,' she returned, and swallowed her coffee.

Fiona's room had a balcony which looked across to the sea, while Chippy's faced the mountains. Both were thickly carpeted and furnished in the modern style. Both had a bathroom adjoining. This idea had pleased the children no end, but their faces now were glum as they sat on Fiona's bed watching Helen close the shutters.

'Do you think he's horrid, now you've seen him?' Chippy asked, looking down at his feet as he swung his legs.

'You'll get used to him,' was all she said in answer to that. 'Come, Chippy, to your own room; Fiona's getting undressed.'

'Oh, all right.' He slid off the bed and obediently left the room.

'How long are you staying?' Fiona asked a few moments later as she looked up at Helen.

'Two weeks – if your uncle doesn't mind having me.' She pulled up the sheet and tucked it around Fiona's shoulders. 'Will you need a blanket?'

'I want lots of blankets.'

'No, one will do.' Helen fetched one from the cupboard in the bathroom and placed it over her. 'It's very warm here; you won't need anything more than this.'

'I think I'd like it if you were staying with us, for a long time.'

'That isn't possible.' On impulse Helen bent and kissed Fiona's cheek. 'Good night, Fiona dear, sleep well.'

They were sitting under a brightly-coloured umbrella, on the harbour at Kyrenia. Numerous small craft were moored and, their drinks finished, the children left the table and went closer to look at them.

'Be careful,' Helen warned as they went rather too near the edge. 'Chippy, just come back a little.'

'They're awfully good children,' Koula remarked, as Chippy immediately obeyed. She spoke with surprise, in fact, on several occasions Helen had noticed her surprise when, after some small command, the children had obeyed without argument.

'You sound as if you expected them to be naughty children.' Helen picked up her glass and held it to her lips, watching her companion curiously and at the same time noticing her hesitation. At last Koula said,

'Leon saw them in England once or twice and – well, he didn't seem to find them particularly well-behaved.'

'They have their mischievous moments,' Helen had to admit, recalling one or two occasions on the journey when she had been forced to curb one or other of them, 'but it's a known fact that a docile child is also a dull one.'

'You like children, I can see.' Koula sipped her drink

and, when Helen made no reply, she went on, 'I love children too. Teddy and I want four at least.'

Helen's glance returned to Chippy, who was looking out over the harbour. A yacht was moving, gliding under the shadow of the castle. A sadness swept over her. If only her child had lived, and kept Gregory close, she might have had another child by now ... or even two. She looked at Koula; she did not envy her, and yet. ... Helen frowned and glanced away. No, definitely she did not envy her, entering into marriage with a man she could not possibly know anything about. Oh, she thought she knew this Teddy – but a woman could never know a man until she was married to him. Then all his faults came out, all his selfishness and callousness were revealed – and by then it was too late to do anything about it. No, she did not envy Koula, on the contrary, she pitied her. But for the present Koula was sublimely happy and Helen said gently,

'Where are you going for your honeymoon? You do go away after the wedding?'

Koula's eyes glowed as she nodded. Helen was glad she had asked the question, glad she had forced herself to show interest.

'I wanted to go to Paris – but Teddy has been there. He wants to go to London.'

London ... what a place for a honeymoon!

'And where are you going?'

'London,' and then, as if reading Helen's thoughts Koula hastily added, 'But I have planned the house, planned every bit myself. I have all the modern fittings in my kitchen. I shall like being there.'

'So Teddy allowed you to please yourself about that?'

'The planning?' Koula's chin lifted a fraction. 'Of course I please myself. It's my house.'

'Yours?' Helen blinked at her. 'Your own – you mean,

you are having it built?'

'That's right.'

'But—' Koula was only twenty-two, and houses were expensive to build – too expensive for Trudy and her husband, Helen knew. 'You must be rich,' she added, aware that Koula was waiting for some further comment.

'My father left some money for my *prika*, and Leon has put the rest.'

'*Prika?* You still must have a dowry?'

'Of course.' Koula frowned in puzzlement. 'The Greek girl always brings the house. This is our custom. In England you do not bring a house because you always marry for love, yes?'

Ignoring that, Helen said,

'But, Koula, you've told me that you are marrying for love.'

'That's true, but still I bring the house because my father left the money. Leon has only added to it because prices have risen so much recently. You see, my father must provide for me in case I married a man who insisted on a dowry.'

'What happens if – well, I know marriages don't often break up here, but just supposing one did. Would the house belong to the husband?'

'But no.' Koula looked amazed. 'If my marriage broke up – it won't, of course – I should have the house and Teddy would have to go.'

'I see.' She was being cynical, she knew, but Helen could not help thinking that this was the reason why so few marriages broke up here. Apparently the man was in a rather precarious position. Should he misbehave he could find himself without a roof over his head. There was after all something to be said for this apparently anti-quated custom of the girl having to provide the home as a dowry.

'You said eighty per cent of the marriages here were arranged – were marriages of convenience. This seems an awfully high proportion.' Koula was not attending; her lips parted in a smile and Helen turned to see Leon standing behind her chair.

'True, nevertheless, Mrs. Stewart. Time is slow to change the customs of the east,' he commented coolly, seating himself on one of the vacant chairs and at the same time glancing over to where the children were standing. 'But these marriages of convenience are for the most part highly successful.' He looked at her strangely and there was something in his tones which impressed Helen as having a far deeper significance than appeared on the surface. 'May I get you a drink? Koula, you have not been attending to Mrs. Stewart's needs.'

'We've been drinking,' Helen told him. 'I've only just emptied my glass.'

'You'll have another?' Without waiting for a reply he beckoned to the man and he came over to them. 'What would you like?'

Helen told him and he ordered. They all sat in silence for a while, watching the passers-by. They were mainly Cypriots for there were scarcely any visitors in the town at this time of the year. Some of the Cypriots came in their cars, from Nicosia. It was a usual Sunday afternoon trip, Koula had said. Whole families came, bringing their food and buying drinks from the café across from the harbour.

Her stay was almost at an end, thought Helen with a tiny sigh. She had been here a week longer than she had intended, but when she suggested leaving both Koula and Leon had pressed her to remain a little while longer. She and Koula had become good friends and whenever Koula was free they would come to the harbour to sit and talk and enjoy the sunshine. Koula had also taken Helen around; sometimes the children would be with them, but on several occasions Leon had insisted they go alone.

'You can't be taking them with you all the time,' he had said, and although this meant disappointment for the children Helen soon discovered the imprudence of arguing with anything Leon had to say.

Darkness began to descend and the fiery glow on the sea turned to purple even while they sat there. Helen and Koula and the children had come from Lapithos by bus, but Leon had his car and they drove home in comfort. Sitting in the front beside him, Helen began to wonder how he came to be at the harbour, for he had been in his study, working, when they left the house. Then something Koula said, and Leon's reply, revealed that he had come especially to pick them up, his mother having told him where they had gone. How considerate! He was a strange man, though; Helen had discovered this very soon after her arrival. His attitude towards the children was one of severity; on two occasions Chippy had received a sound smack on the legs and Helen had been infuriated by Leon's action, and yet, when the child had tumbled and grazed his arm, it was Leon who had dressed the wound. She would never forget her own astonishment on that occasion, or the odd sensation that had come over her as she watched Leon with the child. So gentle his fingers seemed, and he himself had wiped the tears from Chippy's face. As for Leon's attitude towards herself, it was ever one of courtesy, but with a coolness and indifference that proved without doubt Brenda's assertion that he had no time for women. The courtesy he extended towards her was all part of the Cypriot tradition; it was met with wherever one went. Nevertheless, his invitation for her to extend her stay was genuine – in fact, he had been most anxious for her to remain a while longer as his guest. Endeavouring to find a reason for this, Helen could only conclude that he was grateful for her help with the children, for Araté had not yet taken over

34

her duties with regard to looking after them.

The road from Kyrenia to Lapithos ran for some way parallel to the sea, and then turned off into the hills. The track wound this way and that, becoming narrower and more stony as they climbed towards the lovely white villa standing out in the pearl and amethyst light of a fleeting dusk. A great sense of peace and solitude came over Helen as she got out of the car and stood gazing over the narrow coastal plain to the sea.

'Excuse me, please. I find it chilly.' With this apology Koula went swiftly into the house.

All around the air was scented; Fiona remarked on it as she came and stood beside Helen.

'I like the smell of the garden, don't you, Mrs. Stewart?'

'Yes, Fiona, I think it's wonderful.'

'Are you sad at going home?' Fiona asked and then, without waiting for an answer, 'I'm sad that you're going.' There was a catch in her voice as she added, 'Can't you stay a little while longer?'

'I've stayed an extra week, dear. I have a home of my own, you know.'

'But you're all by yourself,' Chippy put in, coming over to them. 'It isn't nice to live by yourself. I wouldn't like it at all.'

'Of course you wouldn't,' Helen agreed, smiling. 'But I'm used to it.'

'But what do you do?'

'Oh, all sorts of things. I read and I paint a little—'

'Pictures?'

'Yes, pictures. I quite like being on my own, Chippy, so you mustn't look sad like that.'

'You like living alone, Mrs. Stewart?' Leon had come round from the other side of the car; he was standing on the drive, looking down at her and, it seemed, waiting curiously for her response.

'I'm used to it,' she supplied, but he repeated his question.

'Yes, I like living alone.'

'You don't sound very sure of that,' was his surprising comment, and, after a silence that had an almost electrifying effect on the air around them, 'I wish to speak to you privately, Mrs. Stewart, after dinner, when you have put the children to bed.'

'Privately?' Why this quivering sensation within her? 'Shall I come to your study?'

'If you please; we shall not be disturbed in there.' His tones were clipped, his eyes contained that familiar cold metallic glint, his mouth was set in a hard inflexible line. He waited a moment for any further question from her; when she remained silent he turned and went into the house. Helen followed, in a rather dazed fashion, scarcely aware that the children were clinging to her hands as they skipped along beside her.

Although filled with curiosity, and even aware of an odd tingling sensation that had the effect of making her heart beat faster, Helen was totally unprepared for what Leon had to say as she entered his study later that evening. After bringing out a chair and inviting her to sit down he began, without preamble, and in tones so cool and matter-of-fact that she was completely staggered,

'Mrs. Stewart, I was quite serious when, earlier today, I said that our marriages of convenience are, for the most part, highly successful.' He took a chair himself and calmly sat there facing her. 'During a conversation with you recently I gathered that you are not hoping for a second marriage based on love. I did interpret that correctly?'

'Y-yes,' she stammered, quite unable to remember the conversation he mentioned. If she had said such a thing, it would have merely been in passing, for it was not the sort of thing she would discuss with anyone – except per-

36

haps a woman friend. Besides, she was not hoping for a second marriage at all.

'I thought so. And as there isn't any likelihood of my ever feeling deeply for a woman I'm putting a proposition to you— No, don't interrupt, Mrs. Stewart, wait until I have finished.' He leant back in his chair and although his eyes never left her face he appeared not to be noticing her at all, for his expression was dark and bitter. 'I had word last week that my brother will not recover from this illness – in fact, he cannot last more than a month at the most—'

'The children will be orphans! Oh, but how dreadful—'

'The children have a mother,' he reminded her harshly, obviously assuming that she knew the details of their history. 'However, that is not important, for she is of no use to them now. They'll have to make their home permanently with me – there's no alternative. I've watched you – and them – most carefully – and it is clear that they are just as greatly attached to you as you are to them. This being the case I hope I can persuade you to remain here and care for them—'

'Oh. . . .' She heaved a great sigh and said, 'Is that all? I will certainly consider it—' Helen was silenced by the look he gave her. He said softly,

'I requested you not to interrupt,' and a flush mounted to Helen's cheeks. He waited a moment and then continued, 'As you know, my sister is to marry next month, and my aunt and uncle will be leaving about the same time. In England it would be permissible for you to enter the house of a man and become nanny to his children, even though he lived alone. Here, unfortunately, this would be frowned upon, for we are more greatly concerned with the proprieties than in your country. As you seem to be quite indispensable to the happiness of the children I'm asking you to marry me.'

She had known what was coming, and yet she was stunned into silence. Had ever a proposal of marriage been put with such cool deliberation? she wondered – and after only three weeks' acquaintanceship! He said no more, allowing her time to collect her scattered wits. Still very dazed by his proposal, she was at the same time gradually accepting the fact that marriage was the only way out of Leon's difficulty, for as he had said, in this country a woman could not live in his house without becoming his wife. The servants, Araté and her husband, had their own home lower down the hill, but even had they slept in Leon's house it would have made no difference. In this part of the world a single woman, living in a man's house, no matter in what capacity, would be regarded with extreme suspicion and disfavour, as also would the man himself.

'I – can't marry you,' she managed at last. 'I would have considered coming to look after Chippy and Fiona, but marriage. . . .' She was not sure, for it was true that she had come to care deeply for the children. It was true that they would be desperately unhappy were she to leave them. It had been bad enough before, but now . . . now they had to be told about their father. . . . 'I don't know what to say, Mr. Petrou,' she murmured, staring across at him with eyes that were now far too bright. 'I – I can't even *think*.'

He was a wise and clever man, Helen concluded as, in a much softer – and even gentle – tone, he told her that he fully understood the conflict she must be experiencing. He did not for one moment expect an immediate decision; she must give the matter some considerable thought, taking into account the advantages both to the children and herself. As for his own part in the marriage, she had nothing to fear from him. All he would ask of her was that she remain chaste and never subject him to humiliation by conduct that could even remotely be described as indiscreet.

'You would have no fear of that—' She stopped, amazed that she should have spoken her thoughts aloud.

Leon smiled at her confusion and the transformation in him was startling. Yes, he was handsome! Gregory had been handsome – and consequently women ran after him.... But if women ran after Leon she wouldn't be hurt, she wouldn't even care. What was she thinking about? There was no question of marriage to him. No, not even for the security, not even for the children, would she contemplate marriage a second time. Besides, Leon had only contempt for women, while she disliked and distrusted men. The idea of marriage between two such people was ridiculous.

# CHAPTER THREE

THEY had been married two months when the miracle of spring came to the island. The winter rains, and meltwater from the mountain snows, had transformed the bare brown earth and everywhere bright green shoots sprang up to clothe the plains, and the mountain slopes were becoming a riot of colour as the wild flowers came rapidly into bloom. From the verandah outside her bedroom window Helen stood gazing dreamily over the narrow coastal strip to the great expanse of sea. The Mediterranean was a brilliant turquoise blue, shading to a lighter colour as it stretched towards the horizon, yet it remained dark enough to contrast sharply with the paler blue of the sky.

'Aunt Helen!' A swift smile touched Helen's lips as she moved to the rail and looked down into the garden. Fiona was standing there, her glowing face turned up, a satchel slung over her shoulder. 'I'm back.'

'I can see that,' laughed Helen. 'Are you hungry?'

'Faminous!'

'Ravenous, you mean.'

'Yes, that's right. Have we any of those cakes you made yesterday?'

'A few. I'm coming now; I'll see what we have in the tin.'

Turning into the bedroom, she caught sight of herself in the mirror. Old-fashioned, Trudy had bluntly said when Helen had visited her last week.

'Why the pose, now that you're married? You'll not hold him, I'm warning you. It doesn't take much for these Cypriots to stray. A pretty face, and they're lost . . . unless they have something better at home.'

'Are you talking from experience?'

'Certainly not. My Tasos is different— Oh, yes, he is, so you needn't laugh! But the general run – well, as I say, I'm warning you, because you're my friend. You're beautiful, Helen, so why this severity? And what about the length of your clothes? – heavens, I can't even see your knees!'

'Aunt Helen. . . . Where are you?'

'I'm coming, darling.'

Fiona was in the kitchen, walking around, her satchel trailing on the floor behind her.

'Where are the cakes?'

'Put your satchel away— No, hang it up where it should go, please.'

Grinning mischievously, Fiona went out to hang her satchel in the cupboard in the hall. Then she came and sat down at the kitchen table, swinging her legs from the high stool and waiting expectantly for Helen to produce something to eat. Helen stood looking down at her for a moment, recalling the child's reaction when Leon had told her and Chippy about their father – after his death. Her sweet little face had remained frozen at first, and then she had sobbed piteously on Helen's breast. Chippy, his lips tight, had tried valiantly to be brave, but eventually he too had broken down. This heartrending scene, and the dark expression of anxiety in Leon's eyes, had proved too much for Helen. Her decision was impulsive, she told herself, resulting from a strong emotion that was only temporary. She would come to regret the marriage, for to live with this dark and austere foreigner, whose way of life and customs were so different from her own, could not possibly be pleasant. Robert had firmly asserted that no Cypriot could live without a woman, and although this aspect of his private life would never touch her, she would always be aware of the existence of these women, and this could scarcely make for contentment

41

and peace of mind. Despite her many inner warnings, Helen had allowed compassion to overrule them, and she still had no regrets. This type of marriage suited her. There was no involvement of deeper feelings, no awakening of emotions and, therefore, no risk of disillusionment a second time.

'Aunt Helen – oh, do be quick!'

Laughing, Helen went to the cupboard and produced the cakes. Then she poured a glass of milk.

'Where's Chippy?' she asked, as Fiona filled her mouth with cake. 'Why is he always later than you?'

'He's with some boys. He can talk to them, but I can't. It's hard, learning Greek, but the teacher's kind; she tells me all the words.'

'And you promptly forget.'

'I remember some of them – but the letters are so funny. Why do they have them upside down?'

'They're not upside down; they're just different from ours, that's all. You'll soon learn the language.'

'But you told Uncle Leon you'd never learn it.'

'I'm older, and it's always harder to learn when you're older. I expect I shall eventually learn enough for my needs. It isn't all that important; most people here speak English.' Helen glanced at the window as Chippy appeared on the verandah. He came through the glass door and a moment later his satchel went spinning across the polished floor.

'What's Fiona eating? Can I have some?'

'When you've put that satchel away.'

'Hang it up for me, Fiona.'

Helen's eyes opened wide.

'What did you say?'

'I told Fiona to hang my satchel up.' Chippy eased himself on to a high stool and sat there, waiting to be served with cakes and milk.

'Take your satchel away,' said Helen sternly. 'At once.'

'Fiona—' Gesturing with his thumb, Chippy indicated the satchel.

'I'm not hanging your bally old satchel up! Do it yourself!' Fiona took a long drink and then filled her mouth with cake again. 'I don't know what's the matter with you, Chippy, you're always trying to boss me about.' She looked up indignantly at Helen, emptied her mouth, and said, almost fiercely, 'He asked me to clean his shoes this morning—'

'Clean his shoes!' Helen stared at him unbelievingly. 'You asked your sister to clean your shoes?'

'That's right,' replied Chippy calmly. 'Sisters always wait on their brothers here. It's the boys who are important; the girls just do the work and – and everything,' he ended vaguely.

'And who, might I ask, has been telling you all this?'

'The boys,' supplied Chippy airily. 'All their sisters wait on them. I felt silly when I said my sister didn't wait on me, because they all laughed and said I was a sissy.'

'I don't believe they used that word.'

'It was another word, in Greek, but it meant the same.'

'Well, sissy or not, you're to clean your own shoes. Now go and see to that satchel.'

'But you don't understand, Aunt Helen—'

'What doesn't Aunt Helen understand?' Leon stood in the doorway, tall and slim and immaculate in a cream linen suit. Although he spoke to Chippy his eyes were on Helen. They flickered over her from head to foot; for the first time she felt conscious of her drab appearance. She wore a skirt and sweater, both dark brown in colour; her fair hair was drawn tightly back and fastened in the nape of her neck with a plain tortoiseshell slide. Her stockings were thick and her shoes heavy. His attention returned to Chippy. 'Well?' His voice was stern and Helen wondered if he had been listening to the conversation before he entered the room. 'Have you suddenly lost your tongue?'

Chippy's confidence and superior air had evaporated. He said almost meekly,

'It's nothing, Uncle Leon.'

Leon turned to Helen and she was forced to answer for the child. She spoke lightly and with a hint of amusement.

'Chippy is fast becoming a true Cypriot. He considers the female to be inferior.'

'Indeed?'

'He bosses me about and makes me clean his shoes.'

'That's a fib,' Helen chided. 'He only asked you to clean them.'

Leon had been listening, Helen concluded, for he evinced no surprise whatever on hearing this. He spoke very softly to his nephew.

'Get off that stool and remove this satchel.' He touched it with the toe of his shoe.

'Yes, Uncle Leon.' Chippy obeyed instantly, but glowered at his sister as she cast him a triumphant glance. 'All the boys at school have their sisters doing jobs for them,' he said when he came back, speaking to no one in particular. But then he added, almost defiantly, 'Aunt Koula did jobs for you. You were always telling her to do things, and fetch things.'

An awful silence followed this little outburst, and then Leon told Chippy to go to his room.

'Oh, no,' protested Helen, already handing Chippy his milk. 'He didn't mean to be rude. The boys have been talking to him, and he now knows it's the custom for girls to wait on their brothers—'

'Chippy, do as I say.' The voice was low and menacing; even Helen trembled slightly on hearing it.

Fiona's rather gloating expression faded. Surreptitiously she stuffed a couple of the small cakes into her pocket, slid from the stool and made for the door, following her brother. Helen noticed her action and, glancing at Leon, she felt sure he also knew what Fiona was about. But to Helen's surprise he allowed his niece to leave the room.

'What has given you the idea that the woman is inferior in Cyprus?' he asked, moving towards the verandah door.

'It's a fact, isn't it?'

'Just depends how you interpret the man's attitude towards the woman,' he told her, once more looking curiously at her, his whole interest this time on her face. He was examining every curve, every line, it seemed to Helen, and she moved to the table, taking up the plate and glass lying there, and carrying them to the sink. 'In your country the woman is equal, but in gaining this equality she appears to have lost something far more precious.'

Turning, Helen regarded him questioningly.

'What has she lost?'

'She often receives neither respect nor courtesy – but more than that, she is not regarded as a *woman*; by this I mean she is not treated with care by the male sex – is not cherished.'

'Cherished?' Amazement now in her wide blue eyes. These were not the words of a woman-hater. 'I have not been given to understand that eastern men cherish their wives.'

'Then you've been misinformed. We cherish all our women – I am speaking generally now, of course, but there is always the exception. Some men here are not kind to their womenfolk, but these are in the minority, I can assure you.'

'I don't know how you can say this. From what I have seen women here are merely servants – vassals, almost.'

'Nonsense!' He was actually angry, for his voice was

45

sharp. 'Women work in the house because it's natural for them to do so. The man brings in the money.'

'Women work in the fields,' she said, placing the glass under the running tap. 'I've seen them often.'

'True, but the men work alongside them.' He stood in the doorway, one hand resting on the jamb, and for a moment his attention was on the view. There was a dramatic quality to the light, owing to the position of the sun and the brilliant blues of sea and sky. The sprinklings of grey in Leon's hair were picked out; they shone like silver. Helen glanced away, reaching for a towel to dry the glass. 'The women enjoy working in the fields; they like to be out of doors.' He turned his head, watching her as she reached up to place the glass on a high shelf. Her dress came up and when she turned he was glancing at her legs. They were shapeless in her thick brown stockings. He changed the subject, saying unexpectedly, 'Helen, you're not short of money?'

'No – no, I've plenty.' Swift colour touched her cheeks, but her eyes held faint surprise. His allowance was generous. He must know she was not short. He shrugged on reading her expression.

'I just thought I'd mention it, that's all,' and then, 'You have only to ask; you won't find me mean.'

Her eyes widened. Was he hinting that she should buy some clothes? Well, she did not intend doing so. There had been occasions recently when his dark eyes had regarded her with an expression that had brought her a tinge of uneasiness, had for some reason reminded her of Robert's statement that no Cypriot could live without a woman. Leon was out nearly every night, and Helen had her own ideas of what he was doing. But there were times when he would remain at home for a whole week. As yet she herself had no attraction for him, but she wondered how his mind worked. She concluded that one woman was much the same as another to these passionate eastern

46

men ... and the time might just come when— Helen dismissed the thought. Life was pleasant; she had the children, and a beautiful home. There was no sense in complicating her life by running the risk of awakening any desires in her husband. No, she was unattractive to him – and she intended remaining that way.

'You're not going to keep Chippy in his room too long, are you?' she asked in a faintly pleading tone. 'He's new to all this, and he listens to the other boys. He's just at the age when he wants to feel important.' She went towards him and Leon moved aside in an unspoken invitation for her to come on to the verandah. She smiled and stepped out; he stood beside her and she was conscious that her head barely reached to his shoulder.

'You're far too lenient with them,' he said, and although his voice was stern Helen was left with the impression that he was not in fact complaining about the way she handled the children.

'They're so young – and they've had this shock.'

'But they've readjusted remarkably well, and quickly, too.' His firm lips curved in a smile and the metallic light suddenly left his eyes as he added, 'You're good for them, Helen. No, I won't leave him too long; but he must learn that he can't treat his sister as an inferior. He must realize that we expect him to care for her.'

She glanced up quickly. What a strange man! Could he really be a woman-hater? Certainly his brother's experience had affected him, for hadn't he said, when about to propose marriage to her, that he would never care deeply for any woman?

Helen reflected on his attitude towards her since their marriage. It was both courteous and friendly, though at times markedly cool. But not once had he spoken harshly to her; never had he given her an order or adopted an air of superiority towards her. There was no excuse for his doing so, of course. He had asked her to marry him and

47

she had obliged. It was her right to expect to be treated as
an equal. Nevertheless there was always present that arrogance, for it formed a permanent part of his make-up.
At times its presence could be felt, profoundly. At others
it was scarcely discernible. She looked up at him again,
noticing the firm line of his jaw and the faint movement
of a muscle at one side of it. The smile had faded and his
mouth was set, set in the familiar taut line that produced
the harshness which tended to mar his otherwise excep-
tionally handsome features. What was he like when he was
really angry? What would he be like were he crossed or
defied? Allowing her eyes to stray to his mouth again,
Helen felt an odd tremor pass through her and she found
herself hoping fervently that there would never be an
occasion when she would cross him – for she was suddenly
convinced that he could actually be cruel. Sensing her
interest, he turned, and glanced down at her in-
quiringly.

'What time can Chippy leave his room?' She spoke
with the haste of confusion . . . and wondered why.

'Some time before tea. I shall see.'

'Before tea? But it's only half-past two.' Here the
school day started at eight in the morning and ended at
two in the afternoon. 'You won't keep him there another
two hours, surely?'

'Not two hours, no. But he will remain there for a while
yet. He won't take any harm.' His tones were quiet, but
Helen knew he would brook no further discussion on the
matter and she fell silent, watching Fiona in the garden
below. She was playing with the stray dog that had recently made its home with them. There were numerous
stray dogs in Cyprus; they lived both in the towns and
the country and it was a puzzle to Helen how they managed to obtain food. When this lovely golden Labrador
had settled in their garden Helen expected Leon either to
send him off or have him destroyed. Instead, he ordered

Araté to feed him and find him a basket in which to sleep.

Leon moved, stooping slightly to lean over the rail as he too watched his niece with the dog. Yes, mused Helen again, he was a strange man in many ways, an enigma with contrasting traits to his character. Hard and un-yielding at times, especially with the children, he could yet extend sympathy to this homeless animal. His attitude towards women, too, was strange. Although interested in them for one reason only, he had not allowed even a hint of disparagement to enter his voice when speaking of them. With his mother he had been gentle, with his sister, generous. But on the one occasion when he had referred to the children's mother his tones were so harsh that Helen could almost imagine his being capable of murder. She glanced at him now in profile and hoped again that an occasion would never arise in which she would ever cross him.

But that very evening there was a clash of wills, and for the first time Helen felt the impact of his forceful per-sonality. She had arranged to visit Trudy once a week; this meant her being out when the children came home from school and Helen felt she must mention this to Leon.

'They'll be all right with Araté – just for about an hour? I'll be home just after three.'

'Of course.' Leon was spending the evening at home and they were sitting on the verandah, drinking coffee and chatting. 'What time are you going?'

'I'm leaving here about nine o'clock.' She had seen Robert in the village yesterday and he had mentioned going into Nicosia to get some paints and canvases. On learning that Helen was also going to Nicosia he had nat-urally offered her a lift, and she had accepted.

'Nine?' A slight frown touched Leon's brow. 'If you could make it earlier I could take you.'

'That's all right, Leon,' she smiled. 'That young man I met on the ship, Robert – you know, I mentioned him to you – he's going into town and is giving me a lift.'

Leon's frown deepened. He said quietly,

'I prefer you not to accept a lift. I'm joining the convoy, because I must be at the office very early tomorrow, but I see no reason why you shouldn't come with me.'

'But the convoy leaves at seven-thirty. I'd be there far too early.'

'Then you can stay at the office for an hour or so.' There was a distinct note of inflexibility in his voice; Helen was still bristling slightly from his calm comment that he preferred her not to accept a lift. She would not be told what she must, and must not, do.

'I'll take the lift, if you don't mind. It will be far simpler—'

'I do mind, Helen.' Still his voice was quiet but the tone had become a trifle harder. 'Araté will be here and she can see the children off to school.'

'But I don't want to go out so early.'

'Then I'm afraid you must take the bus – or I can order you a taxi if you prefer it.'

'I'm going with Robert,' she said, her voice calm though the colour had receded from her cheeks. 'As I've said, it's far simpler. It's ridiculous even to think of a taxi when I can have this lift.'

Placing his coffee cup on the table, Leon leant back in his chair and looked straight at her.

'Helen,' he said, very softly, 'either you go to town by one of the methods I've mentioned, or you don't go at all.'

For a moment she could only stare, but her temper was rising and she eventually said, rather more sharply than she intended,

'I'm accepting Robert's lift. I'm sorry to go against your wishes, Leon, but I'm not being dictated to. I'm

English, remember.'

'You're my wife and you'll do as I say.'

'I've told Robert. He'll be calling for me.'

'He's coming here?' He seemed amazed. 'You've actually told him to pick you up at my house?'

'Why not?' Helen had seen nothing wrong in Robert's coming to the house for her, but judging by the expression on Leon's face that sort of thing definitely wasn't done. It was a wonder Robert had not explained this, for he seemed to know a good deal about the way of life here. 'If you prefer it I can phone him and tell him to wait for me in the village.'

'You will phone him, yes, but to cancel the arrangements. I made it clear at the very beginning that I would expect you to act in every way with discretion and not to subject me to any form of humiliation. You are now contemplating an act that would leave me open to ridicule.'

'That's stupid! Why should my accepting a lift from Robert leave you open to ridicule?'

'This is a small village – and in any case, in Cyprus everyone concerns himself with his neighbour's business. I'm not willing to have my wife's name linked with that of this Englishman.' There was no mistaking the inflexibility in his voice now, and even in the soft and subtle light from the lamp on the wall above him his face wore a harsh and arrogant expression. Loath to accept his decision, Helen was at the same time convinced that further argument would not only be futile, but would also result in her own humiliation. Leon would have his way, always . . . and not only in a situation like this. She stared at him, knowing again that strange uneasiness which she had experienced on several previous occasions. This uneasiness brought caution; she no longer persisted in opposing his will.

'If you feel so strongly about it, then I'll do as you say

and cancel the arrangement.' The colour had left her face; she knew she looked sallow in the half light. Leon's hard eyes flickered over her without interest.

'You'll come with me?' he asked, and she nodded. 'We shall have to be up very early. I'm sorry about that, but it can't be helped. I have a heavy day tomorrow and this early start will help me to catch up with my work.'

The morning air was bright and clear and the sun shone down brilliantly from a cloudless sky. The car was a great black Mercedes; Helen relaxed in her seat, surprised that she was actually going to enjoy the journey. Once out of Kyrenia they joined the convoy. There were numerous vehicles – lorries, buses and private cars. The number of their car was taken and after only a slight delay they were on their way, escorted by the jeeps driven by the blue-uniformed troops of the United Nations. A huge poster told the travellers that the Turks wanted their 'Freedom, Security and Rights'. All was peaceful; apart from the occasional look-out post and the warning that the taking of photographs was prohibited, there was no indication that the road was in any way controlled. Casting a sideways glance at her husband, Helen saw that his face was tranquil. He portrayed no sign of resentment that he was in this long line of traffic, forbidden to over-take.

'It seems such a pity that there's trouble,' she murmured, catching her breath at the beauty around her. This was truly the 'enchanted isle of Venus'; disunion seemed so out of place.

'It will resolve itself,' Leon returned calmly. 'We're all Cypriots; there's no reason why we shouldn't live together in peace.' Helen remembered that his sympathies were with the Turks, and again she wondered at the peculiar personality of this man – this husband of hers who was still almost a stranger. They were soon passing

52

through the northern range of mountains, formed by violent earth movements that had crushed and distorted the original beds of limestone and thrust them up into massive grey peaks on top of which stood the castles of St. Hilarion, Buffavento and Kantara. The slopes of the mountains were clothed with cypresses and olives, while lower down a riot of colour blazed as the glory of the Cyprus spring unfolded. On the great plain of Messoria the bare and arid land through which Helen had passed on her way to Kyrenia in November was lush and green with wheat and barley, while every now and then there would appear the contrast of brilliant red as a mass of poppies raised their heads above the grain.

With the roadside message 'Welcome to the Free Sector' the convoy split up and each vehicle took its own course. Leon increased his speed, passing heavily-laden donkeys, peasant women with great baskets strapped to their shoulders, and the odd motor-cycle, sometimes with a girl on the pillion, riding side-saddle and looking exceedingly unsafe. Left behind were the goats on the mountainside, and the shepherds tending their flocks of brown, long-haired sheep.

'What are you going to do?' Leon inquired as they reached his office. He brought the car to a halt and turned to her. 'Is it too early for you to go to this friend?'

'I think so. I'll stay here for a while – if it won't be of any inconvenience to you.'

To her surprise he smiled at that.

'I said you might stay,' he reminded her and, coming round to her side, he surprised her even further by opening the door for her. 'We'll have some coffee.'

'It doesn't matter about coffee. I know you want to get on with your work.'

But he insisted. The man who had driven Helen and the children from Limassol was already there. His name was Theophilos; he grinned when Leon told Helen this and asked her to call him Theo. On instructions from Leon he went out, returning a short while later with the coffee on a tray – two tiny cups, each with the inevitable glass of iced water. Helen sat on one side of the desk, Leon on the other. He watched her oddly as she sipped her coffee. She had chosen a dress of cotton, but it was plain and dark, accentuating the lack of colour in her cheeks. Leon said, with what seemed to Helen a touch of caution,

'Are you doing some shopping while you're here?' and again she wondered if he were hinting that she should buy herself some clothes.

'There's nothing I need,' she said, but immediately added, 'Both children require socks; I might get those if Trudy and I go into the town.'

He made no comment and a few minutes later he was removing the tray from his desk. He took a folder from a drawer, but before he began working on its contents he glanced again at Helen and, reaching for a newspaper, was about to hand it to her when he realized his mistake and immediately put it down again.

'I don't expect your Greek will run to that yet awhile,' he said, smiling, and handed her the *Cyprus Mail*.

An hour and a half later Theo drove her to Trudy's flat. He would call back for her at four-thirty, Leon had told her as she left the office.

'The children,' she had protested. 'I can go back earlier, on the bus.'

'They'll take no harm,' he said. 'Have a nice day, and enjoy yourself.'

The road in which Trudy lived was lined with white villas, bungalows and flats. Palms and cypresses grew in many of the gardens, towering over the shiny-leaved orange and mandarin trees. All the gardens were bright with flowers; they grew in pots everywhere, and from the balconies climbing plants wove themselves about the wrought-iron supports and trailed to the ground below.

'I've had to close the shutters,' apologized Trudy as she came to the door to meet Helen. 'The sun fades everything.'

'I haven't yet become used to shutting the sun out. It seems all wrong.'

'I know. I was like that at first; we get so little sun in England that we wouldn't think of shutting it out.' She led the way into the room on the front. For the present this was in the shade and the shutters and windows were open. 'We'll sit in here – it's not as elegant as the sitting-room, but it's cooler at this time of the day.'

'I think it's elegant,' said Helen, sitting down by the window. 'I love this flat of yours.'

'I don't expect it's anything to your house, though.' Something in her tone brought a faint flush to Helen's face. This was her fourth visit to Trudy's flat, and she had not yet asked her to come to Lapithos. 'What would you like to drink?'

'I'll have orange, please.' Watching Trudy as she brought in the drinks a few moments later, Helen thought how slender and lovely she was. I used to be like that, she mused, allowing her mind to wander back to those days when she and Trudy had been in their teens. All the boys had been attracted to them; they could have had their choice. With Helen it had been love at first sight when she met Gregory. They both began eagerly to save and were married two years later. Looking back now it seemed to Helen that her husband's ardour had soon waned. But they had drifted into a comfortable relationship and Helen was happy, if not deliriously so. That first blissful period never lasted, she had been told, many times, and although regret for its loss troubled her for a while, Helen adapted herself, and when their child was born she experienced and enjoyed that wonderful fulfilment that comes to a woman only with mother-hood.

In her deep sorrow at the loss of their baby Helen had looked to her husband for comfort, hoping he would come close to her again, as in the beginning, but their relationship remained the same, comfortable, but unexciting.

Trudy had been much more fortunate, for she and Tasos were as much in love now as when they were first married. Devoted to his wife, Tasos never went anywhere without her. He would never be seen, in the company of a dozen or so associates, sitting in a café playing cards or *trik-trak*. All he wanted to do was get home to his wife, and stay with her.

'Tell me about Leon,' Trudy invited, settling herself down on the opposite side of the window. Her brown eyes were faintly troubled as she added, half hesitantly, 'You've said so very little about your marriage – in fact, you've said practically nothing.'

This was true. Helen gazed broodingly down to the street below, and it was some moments before she spoke.

'I shall have to tell you some time,' she began awkwardly, 'so it might as well be now. Leon and I were married for the sake of the children.'

'Children?' Trudy blinked at her and added, 'Chippy and Fiona?'

'I told you their father died and Leon had to take them. Well, he asked me to remain in Cyprus to look after them. Apparently it would not be the thing for me to live in his house without – without being married, and so. . . .' She shrugged and allowed her gaze to stray to the street again. Trudy waited and Helen was forced to continue. 'That's why I haven't said much about it. It isn't that sort of marriage.'

'That sort?'

56

'I mean ... it's not normal,' Helen managed, and Trudy's eyes opened wide, as well they might.

'What are you talking about?'

Still experiencing difficulty, Helen did at last manage to explain the position, and when her friend continued to stare unbelievingly a note of defiance entered her voice.

'You've always known I'd never again marry for love – I've told you that often enough.'

'You've always said you'd never marry at all,' corrected Trudy. 'So I think I'm to be excused for concluding that, as you have married, it was for love – although I must say I thought there was something odd about it all, for you've been as close as a clam.' She took her glass from the tray, holding it between her fingers and regarding Helen thoughtfully. 'So that's why you've no interest in your appearance? Oh, I'm being blunt, even rude if you like, but you used to be so attractive. Don't you want Leon to fall for you?'

'Indeed I don't,' returned Helen with some feeling. 'I'm still of the same mind as when Gregory died. I'll never let my heart become involved again. This marriage suits me as it is and I mean it when I say that I never want Leon even to notice me.'

Suddenly Trudy laughed, though a trifle apologetically.

'No, it can't be! You read about such marriages, but they just couldn't happen in real life!'

'This one has.' Her embarrassment having dissolved, Helen met her friend's gaze squarely. 'Leon and I are little more than strangers.'

'You never—? No, I can't believe that! Not a Cypriot! He – he just couldn't live like that. None of them can.'

Helen shrugged.

'I know all about how they live. They have affairs.'

'And you don't *mind*?'

'Why should I?' Helen shrugged again. 'As I've said,

57

the marriage is purely a business arrangement. It took place for the sole reason of preventing gossip. No, I don't mind what Leon does. His private life has nothing to do with me.'

'But—' Trudy's expression was still one of disbelief. 'Do you really believe, Helen, that you can go on all your life like this?'

'Why not?'

'It just isn't possible,' said Trudy with firm conviction. 'Not with a Cypriot. He couldn't!'

'What do you mean, couldn't?'

'He could not live in the house with you and not be – be – normal.'

'I've told you, he has his affairs.'

'How do you know this?'

'He goes out every night.'

'Most of the men here go out every night. They spend their time in bars and clubs and restaurants. You can't say he's with women.'

'I believe he is with women.'

Trudy shook her head in bewilderment at the calm indifference in Helen's tones.

'You really don't care?'

'I've told you, there's no reason why I should care. I've no feelings whatever for him.' Helen gave a little inward sigh of impatience. 'You know exactly how I feel about men, Trudy. I've no intention of ever allowing myself to become involved emotionally.'

'Well, I'll tell you this; whether you intend becoming emotionally involved or not, you'll never go on for the rest of your days living in this sort of unnatural state.'

'I see no reason why not,' said Helen, but her friend shook her head.

'Leon is bound to – to—'

'He promised. Besides, he finds me completely unattractive.'

Trudy regarded her for a moment, taking in her attire, her pale cheeks and lips, the severity of her hair style.

'How do you know he finds you unattractive?'

'He never so much as looks at me.' Even as she said that Helen frowned, recalling those occasions when he had looked at her. 'He promised,' she said again, and wondered if it were herself she was trying to convince.

'Promised!' Trudy had to laugh. 'Do you honestly believe he'll keep to his word?'

'I think he's to be trusted,' Helen returned, and a rather pitying expression crossed her friend's face.

'How little you know. I shouldn't set much store by a promise like that if I were you. These eastern men are what they are – or what the climate makes them. I'm married to one, so I should know. I'm sorry to disillusion you, but you're making the biggest mistake of your life if you think you're going to keep your husband at arm's length indefinitely. Men just aren't made that way— Besides, it isn't natural, not for either of you. No, Helen, you can take my word for it, when Leon decides to break that promise he'll do so, without any qualms whatever—'

'But my feelings; he must consider those.'

'Oh, for heaven's sake, Helen! You're not innocent. When a man's in the mood to – to—' She broke off, shrugging impatiently, but after a moment she added, 'When the time comes he'll not even remember making the promise, so you might as well resign yourself.'

To her surprise Helen found herself trembling. She said, rather desperately,

'Leon has these diversions. He'll never want me.'

'You've no actual proof that he does have – diversions, as you call them,' Trudy said, laughing at Helen's way of putting it. 'In any case, it's far more convenient to have what you want nearer at hand. He might not always feel like going out for his entertainment—'

'Please, Trudy!' Helen's face flooded with colour. 'I think we'll change the subject.'

Which they did, and the rest of the day was spent pleasantly for both of them. After a lunch taken on the verandah they went into town.

'Many of the shops close from one until half-past three,' Trudy said as she parked her car down a side street. 'But some keep open. We shall get what we want.'

Helen bought the children's socks and that was all. Trudy was interested mainly in food. Their shopping finished, they went into a café for refreshments. Dozens of pairs of eyes glanced up from cards and *trik-trak* to look at the two girls with interest.

'I hate these cafés,' Helen complained. 'Why do they stare so? Anyone would think they'd never seen a woman in their lives.'

'It's because their own women don't frequent these places, but you'd expect them to be used to us foreigners by now. Heaven knows there are enough of us.' Trudy glanced around. 'Come on, let's go out here.'

They sat on the terrace, lingering over *ouzo* and a *mezé* consisting of olives and cucumber, of small cubes of liver and cheese. Helen recalled her initial difficulty in becoming used to the food.

'Have you been to the Mare Monte?' Trudy asked conversationally, and Helen's eyes lit with interest.

'No, but Robert asked me to go there with him.'

'Robert? Oh, yes, the young Englishman you met on the ship. He goes there? They make a marvellous *mezé* — one of the best I've ever had. Are you going with this Robert?' Trudy asked curiously.

'Perhaps I shall — one of these evenings. It does get rather lonely at times, when I've put the children to bed.'

'You could leave them?'

60

'Araté would stay with them.'

'Leon's always out, you say?'

'Not always, but most nights he goes out.'

Trudy's eyes flickered oddly, then she said, without any attempt at tact,

'You'll have to doll yourself up a bit if you go out with this Robert.'

Helen shrugged and replied unconcernedly,

'I haven't anything to doll myself up in, so I'll probably not go with him, after all.'

On their arrival back at the flat there was still half an hour to go before Theo came for Helen, and Trudy took her into the bedroom to show her some new clothes she had bought when on her recent visit to Egypt.

'I still think English clothes are the best I've seen, but how do you like these?' She brought out several dresses and suits. Helen eyed them appreciatively, commenting on Trudy's good taste.

'Thanks – but I slipped up with this one,' Trudy confessed, bringing out a dress in blue linen. It was low cut at the neck and very short. 'It doesn't suit me at all. I saw it in the window, knew it was my size, and bought it without trying it on. Tasos hates it.'

'But it's lovely,' protested Helen, taking it from her. 'I'm sure it suits you.' She held it up against Trudy and then had to admit that her friend was right. 'It's the colour; it's not the right shade of blue.'

'More your colour,' Trudy said. 'Hold it up against you.'

Helen did so, and automatically moved towards the mirror. No doubt about it, her whole appearance was changed.

'Yes, it is my colour,' she admitted, and put the dress down on the bed.

'You can have it,' offered Trudy. 'It's no good to me.'

'Oh, but you'll wear it some time – no, it's good of you,

Trudy, but I wouldn't dream of taking it. Why, it's brand new.'

'I wouldn't offer it to you if it weren't.' Trudy picked it up and held it against Helen again. 'It's you – yes, you must have it.'

Helen shook her head, but feebly. The dress was simple, but well-cut. It certainly did something for her.

'I'd have no occasion to wear it,' she began, when Trudy put in,

'You can wear it any time. What about this outing with your friend Robert?'

'Well . . . I haven't definitely decided to go. . . .'

Helen was standing on the steps, the box under her arm, when Theo came for her with the car.

'I'll see you next week – do come, won't you?'

'Yes, I'll come – and thanks a lot for the dress.'

'You're welcome.'

'I wish you'd let me pay for it—'

'Not all that again, please!'

'All right,' Helen laughed and, a moment later, waved to her friend from the car.

'Goodbye,' Trudy called. Then, on a strangely cryptic note, 'And the best of luck!'

# CHAPTER FOUR

The air was filled with the fragrance of orange blossom. The last golden rays of the sunset spread from the west to the rugged heights of the Kyrenia mountains, setting them aglow with the pale embers of a dying fire. Over the wide expanse of sea violet clouds were sailing. Swiftly the twilight came down; swiftly darkness fell and the moon's lustre began to brush the tiny wavelets, edging them with a silver radiance.

Leon stood leaning in the doorway of the verandah, looking out to sea, his dark head thrown back. Helen joined him there, having seen the children to bed. He moved aside and although his face was in the shadows Helen sensed his smile as she passed him, stepping on to the verandah.

They sat for a while and then Leon reached up to turn on the light.

'What will you have to drink?'

'Nothing, thanks.'

He went into the house, returning with a crystal decanter and two glasses. Helen did not argue when he handed her the drink. But as he sat down again she said,

'Aren't you going out?'

'Not tonight.' He was looking straight at her and she felt her heartbeats quicken. Why was he staying in? He had not been out for almost a week. She knew why her heart was acting strangely, why there was a fear within her. Ever since Trudy's firm assertion that Leon would break his promise Helen had been watching him, trying to fathom every glance, hoping as each day ended that he would go out.

63

'It's a beautiful evening,' she murmured, unconsciously coaxing. 'It's a shame to be in.'

'We're not in.'

'I didn't mean me. I thought – well, you've been in the office all day. . . .'

'You're right – and it was hot and stuffy, for something's gone wrong with the air conditioning.' A pause and then, 'Have your drink and we'll go for a walk.'

The glass was touching her lips; her whole body suddenly quivered. This was not what she wanted.

'Surely you'd prefer to be out with your – your friends.'

'I wouldn't be here if I did.'

Those words had the effect of increasing her trepidation. She drained her glass too quickly and felt her head spin.

'I've a headache.' Mechanically she put a hand to it.

'I'm sorry.' His tones were as coolly courteous as ever, but they held a note of anxiety. He rose from his chair. 'The fresh air will cure it. I'll tell you what we'll do, we'll take the car as far as the beach, and then walk along the shore. The breeze will soon clear your head.'

'The children – I can't leave them.'

'I'll tell Araté to stay until we come back.'

'I'd be better in bed,' she said desperately. 'I think I'll go—' No, she didn't want to go to bed! 'Perhaps you're right, the sea air will do me good.'

'Are you not feeling well?' he asked, examining her white face intently. 'Is there something besides this headache?'

Helen managed a smile then, and stood up. She came close to him and swiftly moved away.

'No, Leon, there's nothing wrong with me. And my head – I think I drank too quickly.'

'You certainly did. As you're not used to it you should be more careful.'

64

Once in the car Helen felt more at ease. She was safe, for a while at least.

Leon parked the car on the side and left it unlocked.

'Will it be all right?' she asked as they walked away towards the shore.

'People don't steal here,' was the calm response. 'In any case, there's no one about.' That was true; they were the sole occupants of the beach.

The moon had come from behind the clouds; it sent a great silver streak across the sea. Not a sound anywhere, not the faintest murmur of waves lapping the shore. Helen had never seen a sea as calm as the Mediterranean. She forgot her fear as they walked along, Leon so tall beside her, talking softly now and then, but often lapsing into silence.

'It's so quiet.' She found herself whispering, for she was enveloped in peace. England was a long way off; the tragedy of her life there now seemed unreal. If only she could keep her husband at a distance her life would remain sublimely uncomplicated. Surely he could not find her attractive ... but even as this thought entered her mind she felt his eyes upon her again, and reluctantly she looked up to meet his gaze.

'Is the head better now?'

'Yes, thank you, Leon.' Her words were stilted. She was beginning to experience an awkwardness when in his presence. She regretted having entered into that conversation with Trudy. Until then her fears had been mere murmurings; she had been able to dismiss them, but now they persisted and she wondered how long it would be before her confidence in Leon's promise returned. However, at this moment she knew peace, and her mind was free from fear. It was pleasant to be walking on the silent shore, even pleasant to be with Leon – so long as he too remained silent. It was only when he spoke that she became disconcerted, for if he spoke softly, and with this hint of anxiety she did not know what might be coming next.

'There's a seat farther along,' he was saying. 'We can sit for a while if you like.'

Presently they reached it and, with one of those little actions that were for ever surprising her, Leon took out his handkerchief and dusted the place where she should sit. No doubt about it, courtesy was almost an art with the Cypriot. And Helen found it refreshing, for she had never received these attentions from Gregory, not even during the first months of her marriage. She smiled at Leon's action and thanked him graciously. Then she sat down, her face turned to the sea. From the narrow strip of plain behind came the heady scent of orange blossom. Helen inhaled and then commented on the perfume.

'You should smell the blossom in some places – where the larger groves are,' he said, sitting down on the seat beside her. And then on what to Helen seemed a sudden impulse, 'I'm going to Famagusta next week, and staying for a couple of days or so. I'm having some major alterations done to some of the packing-sheds there, and I want to be on the spot to do a bit of supervising. Would you like to come with me?'

'Me?' Robert had told her about blossom time in Famagusta, and so had several other people. Even the Cypriots themselves closed their eyes when endeavouring to describe it. Helen had hoped to go some day . . . but the thought of going with Leon had never even crossed her mind. 'I don't know. . . .' They would have to stay in a hotel. . . . 'The children can't be left,' she said hastily. 'Araté likes to sleep at her own house, she's told me that several times.'

'Only because her husband sleeps there,' he smiled. 'While we're away her husband can stay at the bungalow – that will satisfy Araté. No, we need not worry about the children; they'll take no harm for a couple of days. And I feel you need the break. I've been a trifle anxious about you lately.'

Her eyes flew to his. He had noticed, then. But he did not guess the truth; he merely concluded she was off colour. And the break would benefit her . . . . Yes, he was a most considerate man, she thought, but remembered also that there was another side to his nature. She recalled, for apparently no reason at all, her previous conviction that he could be cruel.

'I don't know, Leon,' she began again, when he interrupted her.

'What are you afraid of, Helen?' His voice was low but insistent. She wondered if he sensed her confusion as he waited for her to answer him.

'Afraid?' she quivered, and then managed a rather shaky laugh. 'What is there for me to be afraid of?'

'That is what I'm asking you,' he returned softly. 'And you haven't answered me.'

She shook her head, her gaze settling on the sea for a while as she endeavoured to find some convincing reply while at the same time ensuring his not guessing at the truth. For, should he guess the truth, it might just put ideas into his head that weren't there before.

'I'm not afraid of anything,' she lied, avoiding his eyes. 'There isn't anything I could be afraid of.'

'In that case,' came the calm and even response, 'there is no reason why you shouldn't accompany me to Famagusta. I will give you some money and you can get yourself some clothes.'

'Oh, no!' The exclamation was uttered before she had time to think and she added, more quietly, 'I have plenty of clothes, Leon.'

'Have you? Then they must be tucked away in your wardrobe.'

His bluntness startled her, until she remembered that he was, after all, her husband. Strange, she never thought of herself as a wife and, therefore, was not prepared to hear him speak to her in a way that would be quite natural under normal circumstances.

'Dark clothes are much more serviceable when you have children to look after,' she said, fully aware of the weakness of her excuse.

'That's a rather antiquated idea, isn't it?' he commented, his dark brow lifting a fraction.

'I prefer dark clothes.' The moon was masked by the scudding clouds and as Leon's face became shadowed it seemed to take on that harsh expression. His voice, too, had changed when he spoke.

'I prefer light clothes,' he said. 'I'll see all those you say you have, and if they're not to my liking you will go out and buy some more ... some pretty ones, Helen, with colours that match your eyes and brighten those pale cheeks of yours.' Another change in his voice, or so it appeared to Helen as her heart began to pound. She wasn't imagining things – no, there was a low and husky vibration in his tone. 'I can't be attractive to him,' she trembled, but with that conviction came the knowledge that one woman was much the same as another to these ardent men from the east.

'Surely I can wear what I like,' she protested.

'You will wear clothes that please your husband—' He broke off, sensing her distress, and a gentleness entered his voice as he added, 'I shall take you to the King George Hotel – it's the best in Famagusta – and I would like to feel proud of you. You see, we shall be meeting some business associates of mine.'

So that was the reason! Her whole body sagged as a great sigh of relief escaped her. She chided herself for her fears and for allowing her imagination to run riot. For there was no hint of desire in the gentle tones of his voice. How stupid she was! And it was all on account of taking Trudy's words too seriously. Her mind began to dwell on the prospect of a few days in Famagusta. As Leon said, it would be a break, for much as she adored the children, they were a handful, and so overflowing with mischief at times. The work involved, and the responsibility of caring for them, was a complete change from the life to which she had become used since living on her own, and she often felt tired. Perhaps her tiredness added to her drab appearance, she mused, though the idea did not disturb her at all.

'When would we be going?' she asked, amazed to discover she was awaiting his reply with a keen expectancy.

'Towards the end of next week, probably Friday – then we could return on Sunday or even Monday, it just depends on how this work on the sheds is progressing.'

'You do think Chippy and Fiona will be all right?' she murmured anxiously. 'You know, Leon, they won't take to the idea of our being away from home.'

'Certainly they'll be all right. And they won't take any harm at all with Araté and Nikos. As for their not liking our being away, they must get used to it, for I might take you away again, later, to Paphos. I'm thinking of buying some land there.'

'Perhaps we could take them with us,' Helen suggested tentatively. The children would love that, she knew.

'Some time we will,' he agreed, much to her surprise. 'Later on we'll all have a holiday, as a family.'

As a family. . . . A shadow passed momentarily across Helen's face. Whenever she saw a family out, picnicking or on holiday, or even shopping, she experienced the terrible emptiness of her loss. To go away with Leon and the children, as a family . . . that would be wonderful. On impulse she said,

'Can't we take them this time?' Unconscious pleading in her voice, but Leon passed it by as he said in a firm decisive tone,

'Not this time, my dear. I've said this is to be a change for you. It will be neither a change nor a rest if we take those two rascals with us.'

She did not argue – indeed, it would not have availed her anything, for she knew that tone, and respected it. She leant against the hard wooden support at her back and gazed dreamily out to sea. The dark line of the horizon was clearly visible, for the sea shone like silver. Above, the clouds were breaking up, curling into tinsel threads sprinkled with stars. The intoxicating perfume of wild flowers drifted down on a soft mountain breeze, mingling with the stronger, much headier scent of the orange blossom.

'There's no time like spring,' she murmured huskily, her glance straying along the coast to where, a little distance away, a row of palm trees marked the skyline, waving gently and casting shadows on to the silver-tinted wavelets silently lapping the shore.

'Here it is especially delightful, but unfortunately it's very brief. Summer on the other hand is long. Our winter – if you could call it that – is short, as you know.'

In less than four months she had seen the fleeting autumn, the winter and now the spring. For the rest of the year it would be summer, a summer of glorious sunshine and clear blue skies. The wild flowers would disappear with the baking of the earth, but in gardens and parks the more sophisticated varieties would bloom throughout the whole of the summer.

A cool breeze began to blow up from the sea; Leon turned and inquired if she were cold.

'Shall we go back to the car?' It was still quite early and, despite her previous reluctance to come out, Helen now had no desire to hurry back.

'It's rather chilly now, but I love it here.' She turned up her face and smiled. 'Can we stay a little while longer?'

'Only if you're not feeling the cold,' he began, and

then, with sudden decision, 'No, you are cold. Come on, we'll make our way back to the car.'

But on the way home he turned off the road and pulled up at a low white café. It was brilliantly illuminated with coloured lights and its long wide balcony faced the sea. To Helen's surprise and delight there were several English people seated at the table to which Leon led her. Instantly they smiled a welcome and one young man moved swiftly away to fetch two more chairs.

'Leon, how good to see you! We all concluded you were – er – hibernating since your marriage.' The man who spoke was tanned and bearded; another artist, Helen said to herself even before Leon introduced him to her.

'Phil's not been acclaimed yet, but he will be,' Leon said, laughing at his friend's glance of protest. 'He's good, Helen, and one day he'll put Lapithos on the map.'

'Lapithos is on the map,' flashed another young man indignantly and, turning to Helen, 'We have a nice little community of artists here – but you probably know?'

'I've heard about them,' she returned, smiling. 'I met one of them on the ship coming over—'

'Robert, yes, he talks a lot about you! He's doing fine now, has his pictures in all the souvenir shops on the island. Yes, by Jove, he did mention you – likes you a lot!'

A smile of pleasure transformed Helen's face; she turned impulsively to her husband . . . and the smile froze on her lips. What had she done? His face was dark and scowling. Swiftly she lowered her eyes and to her relief she heard Phil ask Leon what he was drinking. A bottle of the local wine was produced by the smiling waiter and a glass was put before Helen. She glanced up unhappily, bewildered not only by her husband's attitude, but also by her own reaction to it. He often scowled, especially at the children, so why should she take it so seriously this time? The scowl had faded, but his eyes held censure. Again she asked herself what she had done. More introductions took place and soon everyone, including Leon, was in a gay and friendly mood. Covert glances by the women present were cast at Helen and she knew they were wondering what the handsome Leon Petrou had seen in her. His choice must seem all the more puzzling on account of his reputation for disliking women. If such a man did fall, it was usually for a devastatingly lovely woman, someone he just could not resist. And here was Leon, married to a frump.... Helen could read their thoughts without any effort and as she caught her husband's eyes regarding her critically she felt he must be thoroughly ashamed of her. But why bring her here to meet his friends? There had been no necessity for his doing so. He smiled suddenly and for some quite inexplicable reason her heart lifted and for the next hour or so she was as gay as anyone, forgetting her drab appearance as she chatted unselfconsciously to Phil about his work.

'Robert tells me you paint,' he said after he had told her all about his struggles. He made a bare living, it seemed, but he loved the island and considered the climate and the friendly Cypriots to be worth all the money he might earn in his own country.

'Mine aren't very good,' she returned, flushing as everyone stopped, interested in what Phil had said. 'I haven't been to an art school or had any instruction at all.'

'A true artist paints from the heart,' asserted Jerry. He too lived in Lapithos but worked in Nicosia. His stay on the island was precarious, for every six months his employer had to apply for a work permit for him. One day it would be refused, he felt sure. 'You must let us see some of your work, Helen, we're all interested in one another here, you know.'

'I haven't even seen any of it yet,' commented Leon, lifting his glass to his lips. 'My wife is a diffident artist,

I'm thinking.'

'I haven't done any since coming over here,' she explained, and, with a little laugh, 'I haven't had much opportunity.'

'Works you all the time, does he?' Phil wagged a finger at her and went on warningly, 'These Cypriots are great people, but they're noted for keeping their women right down there—' Turning down his thumb, he indicated the floor; Leon opened his mouth to protest and then merely laughed. 'Don't have it, Helen, your husband's very different from us paupers; he can provide you with a dozen servants if he likes.'

'But then I'd have nothing to do, and I'd soon become bored.' Catching the expression of one of the women, Helen again read her thoughts. Bored? – with a husband like Leon around! Taking up her glass, Helen regarded it wonderingly, aware that the woman's gaze was now fixed on Leon's dark profile. The woman actually envied her! Who was she? On being introduced Helen had sensed a hidden animosity beneath the woman's smile, but had instantly dismissed the idea, and even when she later surprised an almost baleful expression in the woman's eyes, Helen had attached no importance to it, assuming that the woman was having unpleasant thoughts about some matter of her own. But now. ... Who was she? Helen asked herself again, wishing she had paid more attention when Leon made the introductions. She fell silent, dropping out of the conversation in order to listen and try to learn something about the woman. All she gathered was that the woman was an estate agent in Nicosia. Later, however, Helen learned a little more and, in doing so, discovered the reason for Paula's obvious dislike of her.

Everyone had said good night and the cars were moving off the park. Leon had gone towards his car expecting Helen to follow, but it was Paula who did so. As Helen hesitated on the steps, watching them and wondering if perhaps they were talking business, Phil caught at her sleeve.

'It might not be tactful of me to say this,' he whispered, 'but don't trust that one. She and Leon used to be . . . well, friendly, to say the least, and in spite of all the rumours that he wasn't marriage-minded, she hoped one day to become Mrs. Petrou. No need to go into details as to how she took it on hearing he'd married someone else.' He let go of her sleeve as Leon turned, obviously expecting to see Helen standing somewhere about. 'None of my business, I know, and you're probably thinking I'm speaking out of turn, but you're nice, and she's an unscrupulous woman – though she does have an attraction for men – some men, that is.' Phil gave her a little shove and she stepped down on to the concrete. 'Better go; Leon's waiting – but watch Paula Maxwell!'

Yes, the dress certainly did something for her. Helen moved away from the mirror so as to see herself from a distance. Her arms were bare, and the low line of the dress revealed the beautiful curve of her neck. Her fair hair shone and fell in half waves on to her shoulders. The dress was short, though, frowned Helen, casting her eyes downwards. But no matter; her legs were shapely now that she wore these gossamer stockings. Her dainty shoes were of blue kid, and fastened with a decorative buckle of a darker shade.

Her wrap was on the chair; she draped it round her shoulders and, picking up her evening bag, she went out and walked down the hill towards the village. She had not gone very far when the car pulled up and she got in.

'Right on time, eh? Aren't I a good boy?' Robert let in the clutch and the car bumped over the stony track until the road was reached.

'How far is this place?' Helen asked, leaning back in

the car.

'Not too far. You haven't been there yet?' He turned the corner and increased his speed as the road widened. 'I should have thought Leon would have taken you to the Mare Monte. Everyone goes. All the English gather there – and in some of the other places, of course. But this particular place is popular with the English, and Saturday's a great night. I'm ever so glad you could come.'

'We'll have to be back at eleven at the latest,' she said, an unconscious note of anxiety creeping into her voice. 'Leon said he'd be in about half-past.'

'We'll be back, have no fear.' A pause and then, curiously, 'What made you phone me? I didn't think you wanted anything more to do with me after turning down my lift the other week.'

'I explained to you – that Leon did not like the idea,' she said, flushing.

'And now? Why did you phone?' he asked again.

They were travelling on the shore road; the sea glistened in the moonlight. Helen recalled that evening when she and Leon had sat on a seat somewhere along here. And then he had taken her to the café and she had enjoyed herself. She had met Paula Maxwell. . . .

The following day Helen had visited Trudy and together they had gone into Nicosia so that Helen could buy the clothes for her holiday in Famagusta. They had gone by bus as Tasos had taken the car. On alighting from the bus they had had a short walk and, on passing the Hilton, Helen had seen Paula in Leon's car. It had swung into the forecourt and Paula and Leon had gone into the hotel – presumably for lunch.

Why should she care? was Helen's immediate reaction to the little tug of pain she had felt on seeing them. Hadn't she known her husband went about with women? Hadn't she wanted it that way? – wanted him to find satisfaction so that he would make no demands on her?

But it was different when the women in his life were unknown, were vague figures without substance. To meet one of them and then to see her with Leon. . . . To see the car sweep past and have to remain silent, not daring to gasp in case Trudy should question her. All through the afternoon she was encompassed in a misery for which there was no accounting, and when at last her husband called at the flat for her she was forced to smile and pretend ignorance of the fact that, only a few hours previously, Paula had been riding in the car, sitting in this very seat.

'What right have I to object . . . ?' But she wasn't objecting; she didn't care. . . .

'I just felt like having an evening out,' she said at last in answer to Robert's query. 'It gets boring sitting there on my own.'

'Doesn't Leon ever stay in?' And, without giving her time to reply, 'That's the trouble with the men here. They all go out, every night, sitting in cafés and talking to their men friends. The family atmosphere of good old England is something you'll never know. But there you are; you women fall for the dark and amorous male every time. Why, oh, why was I born with hair like this!'

Helen had to laugh, in spite of herself, and she laughed the whole evening, forcing herself to be gay while conscious all the while of something hurtful tugging at her heart. There was a strange emptiness within her, an emptiness she had known before, but which she was experiencing for the first time since coming to Cyprus.

She was glad when it was time to go and as they drove back along the coast road she wished she hadn't come at all. They were about half way home when she felt the bump.

'What was that?'

'Blast! A puncture – or my name's not Robert!'

'A puncture?' Her heart missed a beat. 'Will it take

long to mend?'

'I don't mend it; I change the tyre.'

'Of course. How stupid of me.'

They got out and surveyed the flat tyre, Robert with impatience and Helen with dismay. If Leon should arrive home before her. . . . Why should she be afraid? Araté was with the children.

It was awkward, working in the dark, and Robert seemed to be having all sorts of difficulties for now and then a soft curse would reach Helen's ears as she stood on the verge, her nerves fluttering and her heartbeats increasing with every moment that passed. She moved to the car and glanced in at the clock. Twenty-five past eleven. Well, she couldn't possibly be home before Leon now – unless by some miracle he too had been delayed.

'I'll get out here,' Helen said when at last they were climbing the rocky lane leading up to the house. 'Stop, Robert.'

'I'm not leaving you here in the dark at this time of the night—'

'Robert, please—'

'The damage is done now – if there's going to be a row there'll be one, whether I take you right to the house or not. Though I don't see he has any complaint, not if he's always out himself.'

In spite of her continued pleas, Helen was taken right up to the front door of the bungalow. Leon was standing on the top step and even in the half light his face wore an almost murderous expression.

'Good night, Helen,' Robert called as she began to mount the steps. She turned to call 'good night', but her voice was so husky she felt he could not possibly hear.

Without a word, Leon stood aside to allow her to pass. Once in the hall she turned, opening her mouth to speak, to explain about the puncture, but no words came. They stuck in her throat, for she was actually choking with fear. Why should she be frightened like this? And what right had he to stand there, looking ready to murder her? It was not as though she were really his wife. Leon spoke at last, very softly, asking where she had been.

'We went to – to the Mare Monte – you know it, and we h-had a puncture. . . .' She had been holding her wrap against her, but it now fell from her trembling fingers and she stood there in the dress Trudy had given her. Leon had been about to say something in response to her explanation, but he stopped, his hard eyes roving over her, taking every detail of her appearance. Her bare arms, the low revealing line of her dress; her hair, a mass of flowing gold enchantingly windswept from her long wait on the road by the shore. Her cheeks were flushed, her lips parted in a soft and tender curve. His eyes travelled down to the hem of her dress . . . and went no further. And when at last he raised them to her face again their dark depths held something that terrified her even more than that murderous expression she had encountered on first getting out of the car. She tried to release the tight little ball of fear in her throat, tried to speak. Instead, she stooped and retrieved her wrap, intending to drape it around her shoulders. It was taken from her and flung on to a chair. 'God, he's not human,' she gasped, glancing round desperately as if looking for some means of escape.

'Leon. . . .' Huskily she spoke, wondering if the terror in her eyes was as apparent as that in her voice. 'Leon, I – I have a r-right to go out—'

'And leave the children alone in the house?' he interrupted softly.

'They weren't – I told Araté – I left her here.' She blinked at him, momentarily forgetting her own terror in her anxiety for the children. 'What happened? She *must* have stayed. . . .'

'Araté went home at her usual time. She thought you

78

were in.'

'She couldn't – I asked her to stay.' Her glance was bewildered. 'I would never have left them alone, you know I wouldn't.'

'Whatever message you gave to Araté was obviously misunderstood – you know very well of her difficulty in understanding English.'

'She seemed to understand—' Helen broke off, puzzled. 'How do you know she went at her usual time?'

'I was home at nine o'clock. The light was on in her cottage as I passed, and I saw her.' He paused for a moment and his gaze seared into her. 'When you weren't here I naturally wondered what was wrong. The children were awake, but couldn't tell me where you were, so I went along to see Araté. She had no idea where you were, either.'

Only one thing seemed to register. Leon was home at nine o'clock. Why had he come back so early after telling her he would be late? She had taken it for granted he was staying in Nicosia ... and spending the evening with Paula, but. ... Could it be that he preferred to be at home? On impulse she took a faltering step towards him and looked up into his face with a wide and questioning gaze.

'Leon, if I'd known you were coming home so early, I wouldn't have gone out. Why did you—?'

'Obviously you wouldn't.' His eyes were roving over her lovely curves again and that smouldering gleam had returned to their depths. 'How often do you do this?' he demanded harshly.

'This is the first time—'

'Don't lie! Don't you dare stand there and lie to me! How many times have you been out with this man?'

'It's the first time. . . .' She was trembling again but she contrived to keep her voice steady. 'In any case, I h-have a right to go out—'

79

'You have a right to go out with men?'

'Men?' Despite her fear her chin lifted. 'I went with Robert because – because. . . .' Why couldn't she find the words to tell him that she had thought he was with Paula? 'It's not very pleasant, on my own here – you're out nearly every night, Leon.' Why this humility? Why didn't tell him she would please herself what she did? She was not a child to be questioned about her comings and goings. Why then couldn't she stand up to him? 'I'll go out just whenever I like, and you can't stop me—' Oh, God, what had she said! Why hadn't she practised caution? Every scrap of colour drained from her face and she tried to escape as he moved with a lightning step towards her, but her legs were like jelly and she found herself caught in a crushing and merciless embrace.

'You'll go out with men just whenever you like, will you? And you'll dress yourself up for them, make yourself attractive – but for me – for me you'll look like one of the hags from the village—'

'Leon – please! You don't understand, I didn't try to make myself attractive for any reason other—'

'Other than to arouse desire in your man friend, eh?' His face was close to hers, sinister as the dark embers in his eyes that left her in no doubt as to his intentions. 'Well, you've succeeded in arousing desire in your husband and so you'll take the consequences.' His mouth closed on hers and she struggled against its cruelty. But after a little while she lay passive, crying softly as his lips moved from her mouth to her neck and then to the curve on her shoulder from where he had pushed down the strap of her dress. He held her away from him at last, and noticed the tears on her cheeks. The shock of his attack, and the fear within her, had set every nerve quivering. Her body was bruised and her lips were swollen; she recalled his saying that the Cypriots care for their women, cherish them, and her eyes filled up again. He stared at her, watching the tears glisten on her lashes and then roll down on to her face. The sight of her weeping had a strange effect on him; all anger, all the savagery he had displayed, seemed suddenly to dissolve as, with an almost tender gesture, he drew his finger across her cheek, removing the tears.

'Helen, don't cry.' His lips found hers again and he kissed her gently, soothingly, as if he would erase for ever his cruelty of a moment ago. His action amazed her, but it also gave her hope, and when he eventually released her she looked at him and said,

'Leon, you're not going to – to break your promise?'

A long silence; his eyes darkened as they settled on her upturned face.

'You're my wife, Helen,' he replied softly, and a great bitterness engulfed her.

It was true, a Cypriot could not live without a woman – and any woman would do.

# CHAPTER FIVE

BOTH children looked on glumly as Helen closed the lid of her suitcase and snapped on one of the locks. The other lock was giving her trouble and she bent down to examine it.

'How long will you be gone?' Chippy asked mournfully.

'Only three days at the most.' A hint of amusement touched Helen's eyes. 'Brighten up, you silly little goose, anyone would think we were going away for a month.'

'Three days is a long time,' Fiona grumbled. 'It's not fair. Why can't we come with you?'

'Because Aunt Helen wants a rest. Now run along and leave her to her packing.' Leon was in the doorway, but on seeing Helen's difficulty he came over to the bed. 'Something wrong?'

'Uncle Leon,' Fiona began persuasively, 'can we come with you? We'll be awfully good.'

'I said run along.'

'But—'

'We're taking you another time,' interposed Helen with some haste, noticing Leon's expression change on not being instantly obeyed. The children left the room and Leon stooped to see what was wrong with the lock. His strong brown fingers touched hers and she snatched her hand away. His mouth compressed and he straightened up. And then, deliberately, he took her hands in his and held them in a firm possessive grip.

'No doubt you prefer English men,' he almost sneered, his eyes running over her slender figure, 'but unfortunately you're married to me.'

'Unfortunately—' she repeated the word slowly, em-

82

phasizing it, 'I am.' She made an effort to free her hands, but the steely pressure increased and she was drawn resistingly towards him. 'Leon, must I go with you to Famagusta? The – the children are upset—'

'I have said, the children will take no harm.' He bent his dark head and kissed her on the lips. 'Yes, Helen, you must come with me—'

'For one thing! Can't you do without a woman for three days? What sort of a man are you?'

'I think I have a right to expect my wife to accompany me when I go away.' His voice was soft, but a dangerous glint entered his eyes and little white lines of anger ran from his nostrils down to his mouth. 'You obviously believe you know the reason for my wanting to have you with me, and I shan't trouble to deny it—'

'There wouldn't be much point, would there?' Again she attempted to withdraw her hands, and this time she succeeded, but Leon's fingers slid up her arms and gripped her shoulders.

'Be careful, Helen,' he warned, his eyes burning into her. 'Be very careful. For your own sake, don't drive me too far.' His face was close to hers, lean and harsh. The retort died on her lips; no sense in risking an exhibition of his fury such as she had seen a few nights ago. He kissed her again and released his hold on her arms. 'Have you finished your packing?' He bent to attend to the lock and this time managed to fasten it.

'All I need is in the one case,' she said coldly, and turned away, stepping out on to the balcony. So tranquil the scene of calm sea and sky – and little more than a week ago her own mood would have been in harmony with all this peace around her. But now. . . . This tumult within her, how long could she endure it? She had fully trusted Leon when, on proposing marriage, he had said he would not trouble her; she had not thought for one moment that he would break his word. But he had done so, and without offering her either excuse or apology. He had no feelings other than those of desire, there was no depth to his emotions. Characteristic of all these eastern men, she thought. That was why eighty per cent of the marriages were ones of convenience. Koula had firmly asserted that, should her brother ever marry, his would be one of these unemotional unions. Had he not married me, Helen mused, he would eventually have contracted a marriage like that for, as Trudy had averred, it was far more convenient to have what one wanted nearer at hand. And that was all she was, a convenience. She was here and he was saved the effort of going out to seek his pleasure. Bitterly her mouth curved. Her marriage to Gregory had left a good deal to be desired, but her husband had not made that kind of use of her.

'Have you packed all the clothes you bought?' Leon was standing at her elbow. She looked up and saw with faint surprise that the sprinklings of grey at his temples were more pronounced. 'You're taking what I requested you to take?'

'I've packed what I was ordered to pack. I shan't disgrace you, Leon.'

No sound for a while; at length Leon turned to go and then came back. His mouth was against her ear and his voice was the soft and menacing snarl of an animal ready to pounce.

'I warned you to be careful. You'll disregard that warning to your cost,' and with that he left her standing there, her trembling fingers resting on the rail, her eyes gazing mistily out to the clear sharp line dividing the dark turquoise sea from the purer blue of the sky.

They were on their way immediately after the children had gone to school, Leon having to take the longer route to Nicosia as they were too late to join the convoy. It was a glorious morning, with a slight haze topping the mountains at first but soon disappearing as the sun rose higher in the sky. The mountain scenery was ever-changing with each twist and turn in the road. Sometimes the heights would be bare, sometimes clothed with trees, sometimes dark and sombre, or blazing with colour where the spring flowers bloomed in wild profusion. Often the rugged grandeur was breathtaking; in some areas the intense folding of the rocks had brought the beds into an almost vertical position, producing impressive peaks that contrasted darkly with the vivid blue of the sky.

Once the capital was reached, and left behind, the scenery changed. They drove across the plain on the long straight road, passing tiny settlements which were sometimes no more than a cluster of mud huts, often straggling up a low hill or rise. Close by would be the inevitable donkey, its back laden with an odd assortment of boughs and twigs; and a shepherd might be seen on a distant knoll, lazily tending his sheep and goats.

'We'll go straight to the hotel, and then I'll take you to the old city.' Leon's eyes were on the road; Helen glanced at his profile and then turned to resume her scanning of the scenery. 'You've never been to the old city, you say?'

'No.'

'It's most attractive – has an atmosphere which I consider to be unique.'

'I've been told about its attractions. It should be interesting.' She spoke stiffly and without much expression. Leon turned his head for a second to look at her, but she continued to gaze out of the side window.

'Do you hate me, Helen?' he asked unexpectedly, returning his eyes to the road. 'You didn't used to; we were reasonably happy before – before—'

'Before you made a convenience of me? Yes, Leon, we did get along reasonably well. It could have continued like that indefinitely.'

'You think so?' A faintly bitter smile touched the hard

85

edge of his mouth. 'What of you, Helen – would you have been satisfied with that sort of life?'

'You knew I had no intention of allowing my emotions to become involved – I gave you to understand that the day I explained about Gregory, and the way he'd let me down.'

'You haven't answered my question. Men are human, but so are women.'

'Women are different, especially English women.'

'You have no need to tell me that,' he responded bitterly, then he added, 'But, cold or not, I still maintain they're human. You are not going to answer my question?'

'I wouldn't dream of indulging in – in love-making merely for convenience.'

'Still evasive, aren't you?' He swerved to avoid an elderly woman, dressed entirely in black, her body stooping under the burden of the massive basket strapped to her back. 'I object to the word "convenience", Helen. Please don't use it again.' They were coming into Famagusta; the way was lined with trees. A road sign indicated the left turn for the old city. Leon drove straight on.

'Surely you're not hinting that I'm wrong in my deductions? – that you aren't using me as a convenience?' She still evaded him, but a sharp intake of his breath warned her of his sudden flash of anger.

'I've told you not to use that word!'

'You're full of surprises, Leon,' she said sarcastically. 'I shouldn't have expected you to object to the indelicacy of the word.'

'I'm relieved to hear you admit it's indelicate. I was beginning to wonder at your crudity; it doesn't suit you, Helen.' They were entering the more popular part of Varosha, passing through streets of gleaming white bungalows and villas, each with its enchanting garden bright with hibiscus and jacaranda, with bougainvillea and mimosa. The heady scent of orange blossom wafted through the open window of the car.

'Your flattery overwhelms me.'

'Sarcasm doesn't become you, either. You'll oblige me by avoiding that also.'

Helen turned swiftly.

'Am I not even to be allowed free speech?' she flashed, the angry colour flooding her cheeks.

'Certainly you are – so long as it isn't designed to insult me.'

She fell silent and no further words passed between them until the hotel was reached. Their car was parked, their luggage taken up to their room. It was shuttered against the sun; Helen immediately opened both windows and shutters.

'Why do they do it?' she said, stepping out on to the balcony. The wide expanse of blue Mediterranean faced her, with the golden sands immediately below the window. She became aware of her husband, standing close beside her.

'It's the custom,' he said. 'You're not used to our customs yet.'

Custom. . . . It was also the custom for men to treat their wives as possessions. She turned her head. There was a double bed in the room. Had he asked for it? She had been given to understand that twin beds were the rule in all the best hotels.

'I'd better take out my dresses,' she said on a sudden note of dejection. But Leon made no move to step out of her way and she turned again, leaning on the rail and gazing broodingly out to sea. She felt his arms embrace her and stiffened. He must have known how she felt, and yet he said lightly,

'This could be our honeymoon, Helen.'

'Honeymoons are for lovers.'

'So they are.' Was there a note of cynicism in his voice?

Helen could not be sure. His arms tightened. His lips caressed her hair, then moved down to the nape of her neck. Brushing aside her hair, he placed a kiss on her lovely white skin. For a while she stood in meek resignation and then swung round, the delicate colour tinting her face, reflecting the rising anger and loathing within her.

'Can't you leave me alone! Must I suffer your embraces night *and* day?' Brushing past him, she ran into the room, and Leon turned.

'Helen!' Her name fell involuntarily from his whitened lips; he seemed shocked and his hands dropped to his sides. But almost at once he recovered. His fists were clenched, his eyes dark agates of fury as he advanced slowly into the room. 'If that is how you regard my caresses – as something to be suffered – then the answer's yes. I shall take what I want, just whenever it suits me.'

'You promised.' He stood too close. Anger remained in her voice, but fear filled her heart. If only she could escape from this man – but always the children intruded into any thoughts of leaving him. He knew he held her, held her for as long as the children needed her. 'Doesn't it trouble your conscience that you broke your word?'

'I have no conscience with regard to my relationship with you. You're my wife and I'm breaking no rules when I take what's my own—'

'You have no need to remind me that a wife here is a possession,' she cut in bitterly. She was blinking against the sun and she moved to fling the curtains across the window. For the first time she hated the sun, and the clear skies – in fact everything about this island from which there was no escape. 'But you will not hold me for ever,' she went on, speaking her thoughts aloud. 'As soon as the children are old enough I shall leave you.'

A faint ticking sound coming from the direction of the small table over by the wall provided a diversion; they both listened, Helen puzzled, Leon indifferent.

'You will probably have children of your own long before then,' he said calmly, walking over to the table.

'You would hold me *that way*!'

'I would hold you that way,' he answered quietly, and she looked up, startled. For there was a strange tremor in his voice; it was as if the words were forced from him, as if he experienced the greatest difficulty in speaking them at all. Their eyes met and for no reason at all there flashed through her mind the memory of that painful little ache she had experienced on seeing him with Paula Maxwell that day at the Hilton. To her own amazement that memory erased from her mind all that had just passed and, as if drawn by some power beyond her control, she moved towards him, extending a hand in an unconscious gesture of entreaty.

'Leon. . . .'

He took her hand, holding it firmly, and slowly the colour returned to his lips. All harshness was wiped away by his smile.

'Yes, Helen?' But she could not speak, could not frame words to tell him her thoughts, to describe this tumult in her heart, a tumult no longer born of fear. 'What is it?' The gentle tones were faintly pleading. So out of character, she thought, and something in her responded, even though it was against her will.

'This little holiday. . . . Can we – be happy?'

'Helen.' His stare was unbelieving, and then, gently, he pulled her forward, his strong arm about her waist. 'Yes, my dear,' he murmured huskily. 'Yes, we can be happy.'

He held her a little while, not attempting to kiss her, and appearing afraid to hold her too tightly. An inexplicable sensation of guilt swept through her and she frowned inwardly at it. She spoke quickly, in an effort to put the feeling from her.

'What is that noise, Leon? Is it the wood?'

He shook his head, smiling as he spoke.

'It's an insect, they get into the furniture. We shall have to ask the room maid to spray it.'

'An insect? Really? But how does it get in?'

'The tops of these tables are hollow; it's surprising where these insects can get.'

'I suppose when you have a climate like this you must have the disadvantages that go with it.' She gave him a faint smile. 'Nothing is perfect.'

He took her hands again, and stood staring down at them. And then he looked into her eyes and said, rather sadly,

'No, Helen, nothing is perfect.'

After having lunch in the hotel they drove to the old city of Famagusta. The visit, Leon had said, was primarily for business reasons, but although he drove to the packing-sheds he remained there only a few minutes before returning to the car.

'We'll drive through the orange groves,' he said, slipping into the seat beside her. 'They are something at this time of the year, I can promise you.' And he was right; for what seemed miles the groves stretched in all directions. In addition to the orange trees, there were mandarins and lemons, too. The whole area was a mass of blossom and the air was intoxicating.

'It's wonderful,' Helen breathed. 'Oh, I've never seen anything like it in my life!'

Leon stopped the car and they got out.

'It is rather wonderful, isn't it?' His voice was soft, and his eyes had lost their metallic glint as they regarded her for a moment as she stood there, on the edge of the orange grove, her fair hair caressed by the breeze, her cheeks softly flushed and her eyes glowing. She wore one of the dresses that Leon had made her buy – a flowered cotton that accentuated the youthful curves of her body.

'You're very lovely, Helen,' he said, and her colour deepened. Reaching up, over her head, he broke off a small branch. 'Orange blossom for the bride.' He gave it to her, and all at once he seemed so very young, and even unsure of himself. The impression was fleeting and Helen wondered if she had imagined it. Smiling up at him, she took the lovely scented spray and held it to her face. 'Yes,' he said in soft and gentle tones, 'you're very lovely.'

'Tell me about the oranges, Leon.' They were back in the car; Helen was holding the spray in her hand, putting it to her face now and then in order to inhale the perfume. 'What is your work – in the packing-sheds, I mean?'

'All the fruit goes there, after the harvesting, and is washed and graded.'

'Washed? – every orange?'

'All the fruit is washed before being exported, yes. Women usually do this work. Then the fruit is graded, and packed for export.'

'And you just own the sheds – not the groves?'

'I just own the sheds.'

They drove for a while in silence, under a cloudless sky. The road ran close to the sea and all along one side Helen noticed the high plants growing.

'What are these?' she asked interestedly. 'They look like some sort of cane.'

'Bamboos – these are grown to shelter the orange groves from the sea breezes.' The groves extended almost to the sea; it was obvious some sort of shelter was required. 'These trees here,' Leon was saying, 'are grapefruit. We export a great many to England, as you probably know.' There was a hint of pride in his voice. He was proud of his island, and its products, but all the Cypriots Helen had met were the same. Anything produced in Cyprus was far superior to a similar product from elsewhere.

Leaving the orange groves, Leon turned in the direction of the old city. He parked the car in the square and they went into a café for some refreshment. As usual only men were in evidence, and every eye in the place was turned as Helen and Leon walked in. Having taken a good look at Helen, and a casual glance at Leon, the men returned to their newspapers, their cards and their *trik-trak*.

'Do they play for money?' Helen wanted to know, watching two men close at hand playing the game. Leon shook his head.

'Only for drinks.'

'Don't they have any work to do?' She cast him a puzzled glance and he laughed.

'Still troubling your pretty head about the poor women, working, while the men sit about idling their time?'

'It's true!' she flashed, indignant at the idea of all these men sitting here, doing nothing except play games. But at the same time she coloured at Leon's use of the word 'pretty'. What a changeable person she was; having deliberately made herself drab so as not to appear attractive to any man, she was now feeling happy at the idea of Leon's considering her to be pretty. And what did he think about it all? she wondered, for obviously he had known from the first that she was determined to keep him at arm's length. 'I should hate to be the wife of a poor man here,' she added as Leon eyed her questioningly.

'Would you, Helen?' he said drily, and she bit her lip.

'I didn't mean it like that. I meant I wouldn't like to have been born here, and be poor—' She gave a little laugh. 'You know what I mean.'

'Yes, I know what you mean.' He looked up as the café proprietor appeared with a tray on which were two minute cups of coffee and two large glasses of water. 'But the women here don't really mind,' Leon continued, when the man had gone. 'They're used to it, and as long as they eventually find a husband they're quite content.'

Helen picked up her coffee and sipped it slowly.

'These marriages of – the marriages that aren't based on love – how are they arranged?'

'Quite simply. For example, a young cousin of mine, Pavlos, has recently married a girl from a little village in the mountains. He was approached by the girl's brother, who told him of all her virtues, and said she could bring a house. Pavlos agreed to meet her; she obviously pleased him, for he agreed at once to marry her.' Leon picked up his glass of water and took a long drink, his eyes kindling with amusement at Helen's rather shocked expression.

'Is that all?'

'All?'

'The brother – arranging to – to have her looked over, as you might say. It's awful!'

'It's the normal procedure.'

'But the girl – doesn't she have any say in the matter?'

'Not very much,' he admitted. 'I daresay if she flatly refused the young man chosen her father and brothers would listen, but this rarely happens. You see, the man does the girl a favour by marrying her; she is duly grateful and, therefore, doesn't think of refusing.'

'It sounds a hateful sort of arrangement,' declared Helen with some heat. 'It must be dreadfully embarrassing for the girl.'

'Not at all.' Then he added with the glimmering of a smile, 'It's the custom, my dear.'

Their coffee finished, they came out into the square, where the brilliant sunshine reflected back from the walls of the magnificent Venetian palace. Opposite the palace was another imposing building.

'This is the mosque— As you know, this old city is the Turkish quarter of Famagusta. Would you like to go into the mosque?'

Helen nodded and, taking off their shoes, they entered the lovely building that had once been the cathedral of St. Nicholas, built many centuries ago by the Lusignan kings of Cyprus.

'We'll drive around now,' Leon suggested as they came out of the mosque. He took her to see the Venetian Walls, and the citadel with the famous tower where the story of Othello was played out. As they drove around the city it seemed to Helen that she had seen hundreds of churches, all in ruins.

'Are we passing the same ones over again?' she asked, puzzled, and Leon shook his head.

'There were three hundred and sixty-five—'

'Three— Oh, no, there couldn't be, not in such a small place!'

'It's true. Many of them have disappeared, of course, but a great many are left.' He stopped several times to show her, within one or other of the ruined buildings, the remains of the original murals and mosaics.

'Still here, after all those hundreds of years,' she breathed. 'It seems impossible!'

'The climate helps preserve these things. We have so little rain. In your country they'd have disappeared long ago.'

They drove to the Sea Gate, through which Richard Cœur de Lion had entered the city. They left the car and walked. Helen had not felt so happy for a long while. Leon grabbed her hand when, on stepping on a loose piece of rock, Helen would have slipped. He retained her hand for the rest of the walk.

Much later, back in the hotel bedroom, Helen put her spray of orange blossom in a glass of water. Leon watched her as she came from the bathroom; she smiled at him as

94

she put the glass on the dressing-table.

Leon had invited some business friends to dine with them and they were coming to the hotel.

'Which one shall I wear?' Helen had brought three cocktail dresses and she had them all spread out on the bed. Her question surprised her as much as it surprised her husband. Only a few hours earlier she would not have dreamed of consulting him. Taking one of the dresses up, he held it against her.

'Hmm. . . .' He shook his head and picked up another. 'Let me see this. . . .' The short, full-skirted dress in lime-green cotton suited her to perfection. 'This is the one,' he asserted, and put it back on the bed. Then, gently, he took her in his arms and kissed her. It was the first time she had not stiffened at his touch.

Two of Leon's friends were English, the other a Greek Cypriot.

Yannis was the first to arrive. He stared admiringly at Helen on being introduced and held her hand far too long.

'What will you have to drink?' Leon asked, and Yannis turned to catch the frown upon his face.

'Jealous, Leon? – but no, not of me! I shall drink *retsina,* if you please.' He seated himself on a high stool beside Helen and waited for Leon to get the drinks.

Jealous. . . . Helen stared at her husband, immaculate in a lounge suit of corded linen in an attractive shade of blue-grey. His white shirt contrasted sharply with his dark skin and to her surprise and wonderment she felt a little catch of pride, and because of it a blush fused her cheeks when Leon turned to regard her with a cool and even stare. Jealous? But no, how could there be jealousy without love?

Whatever had caused that frown was immediately forgotten, for Leon and Yannis were at once engaged in conversation, discussing business. Soon they were joined at

95

the bar by Leon's two English friends, Eric and Stephen. They were delighted to meet Helen – she had found that, even though there were so many English settlers on the island, they were always eager to meet new acquaintances from England. Helen commented on this and Eric laughed.

'It's true,' he admitted. 'And yet we're everywhere on the island.'

'There'll be more English than Cypriots soon,' commented Leon without rancour. 'People are getting out of your country to avoid the taxation.'

'And so your husband, and people like him, are making a fortune.' Stephen turned to Helen and grinned. 'Land,' he added briefly.

Land ... and the packing-sheds. Was Leon very rich? she wondered. How odd for a wife to be in total ignorance of her husband's finances. She hadn't the vaguest idea of his income.

After dinner they all went out to a night club; Helen became more and more sleepy and she felt she could have allowed her husband to carry her upstairs when, at three o'clock in the morning, they arrived back at the hotel.

After a late breakfast they came out of the hotel straight on to the beach. The sun was blazing down and Leon suggested a swim.

'Can you swim?' he added, shaking his head slightly as if in wonderment at how little he knew of his wife.

'Yes, I love it.' To her surprise she felt no ill effects from her late night and her face was glowing with health as she walked beside him towards the sea. They swam for a while, then dried themselves in the sun.

'I'll have to leave you for about a couple of hours,' he said when they had had their lunch. 'I've some business to attend to and you'll be much more comfortable out there on the beach than waiting in the hot car.' Was it imagination, wondered Helen glancing at him curiously, or did he really find this business irksome? But no, how could he when it was business that had brought him here?

Nevertheless, he was absent only for an hour and a half and her eyes widened when, on opening them, she saw him standing there, clad only in trunks, so tall and bronzed and incredibly handsome. How long had he been there? – regarding her inscrutably from behind those dark glasses? She sat up.

'You're back early.' A sudden shyness spread over her and she began to trace a picture in the sand.

'Were I to believe the evidence of my eyes I'd say you were glad.' He lay down beside her and stretched his long legs. Then, turning on his side, he leant on one elbow and stared up at her. 'Are you glad, Helen? – or daren't I ask that question?' He did not seem to expect a reply and she continued to trace her picture in the sand. Did he want her to *care* – or merely to be his willing slave? Certainly he wanted something different from the relationship that had existed between them until that rather tender little scene yesterday. He had taken that to which he considered he had a right, but she had given nothing. Amorous as he was, her coldness could not possibly satisfy him. Also, it probably hurt his pride that he had not the power to break her down. For Helen had learned from Trudy that with all Greeks, whether they be Cypriots or not, love was an art, an art in which they knew they excelled.

'The Englishman's a novice by comparison,' Trudy had said, a flush rising. And then she had added bluntly, 'If ever Leon does break that promise you'll think yourself in heaven!'

The recollection of those words brought the colour to Helen's face and Leon chose that moment to reach up and raise her head. His touch was gentle under her chin; oddly, she did not resent the gesture which, somehow, had an element of mastery in it.

'Why the blush, my lovely Helen?'

My. . . . Something tingled within her, but she refused to allow even a hint of indignation to affect this truce that they were observing – observing even though both were profoundly aware that its duration might cease with the end of the holiday.

'I – I was thinking of something,' she murmured, endeavouring to read the expression in his eyes. But they were shielded and all she saw was the merest flicker of his lashes.

'What were you thinking to make you blush like that?' Insistence in his voice, but Helen shook her head. His hand dropped, coming to rest on hers. He held it firmly, preventing her nervous scribblings in the sand. 'It's warm,' he said. 'Shall we go into the water?'

Relieved, she rose at once, and Leon rose at the same time, retaining his hold on her hand. They walked like lovers towards the water's edge, and then stepped into the warm blue sea. Leon went a long way out, but Helen kept close to the shore; eventually she came out and sat there on the hot sand, her eyes on Leon's dark head, away in the distance. He waved to her and she waved back. Such companionship as this was new to her; she had not known it with Gregory. She fell to examining their relationship and with wonder and amazement she realized they had never been really close. What she had considered to be a normally happy marriage had merely been an existence that people often described as comfortable . . . but happiness . . .? Before her mind drifted the picture of Trudy, and her glowing expression whenever she mentioned her husband.

'And she's been married six years,' she murmured wonderingly. 'It can last, no matter what people say to the contrary.' Yes, it was an undeniable fact that Trudy and Tasos were as much in love now as on the day they married.

She was tracing in the sand again when he eventually joined her.

'You must paint for me,' he said, reaching for her hand.

'I'm not very good, Leon.' She allowed herself to be pulled to her feet. Water droplets glistened on his dark body. 'I should have brought a towel – but I didn't intend going in the water.'

'I'll soon dry.' His eyes flickered over her, taking in every detail of her slender figure. 'You're dry already,' he observed, and deliberately pressed the length of his arm to hers. She rubbed herself dry, laughing up at him, and he caught his breath. 'About this painting of yours,' he said abruptly, 'I'll be the judge of whether it's good or not. When we get home you shall paint me a picture.'

'No ... where would you put it? These sort of things get in the way.'

'I shall hang it in my office,' came the soft reply, and Helen felt a tinge of pleasure rise. Gregory had no opinion of her work; in fact, he had said openly that her paintings lacked feeling. She would never sell them, he had firmly asserted. And he had refused to let her have any of them on display.

'Perhaps you'll change your mind when you see it,' she warned.

'I shan't change my mind.'

Why did he want her picture hanging where he could see it all the time? Was it to remind him of his ownership of her? She shook off the idea, for it was ungenerous. Whatever faults Leon had, there was a sincerity about him that she liked and admired. The emotional side to his nature was a thing apart, the force of which had resulted in his casting aside any good intentions he had had when first embarking on marriage with her. The breaking of his promise, and his complete disregard for her feelings, had adversely affected her opinion of him. And yet she

99

knew that, basically, her husband was a good man, a man to be relied upon and trusted. And in spite of his arrogance and mastery, in spite of the dominance and cruelty she had to her cost encountered, there was to his character a certain childlike quality she could have found endearing in happier, more natural circumstances.

They walked slowly back to where Helen had left her beach robe. Picking it up, Leon held it for her to put on and then, turning her round, he began to fasten the buttons. There were few people on the beach, for as yet it was early for visitors, but one or two people from the hotel were sunbathing nearby and Helen wondered if her husband was aware that his attentiveness was being watched with interest by a couple whose table, in the dining-room, was next to theirs.

'Hold your chin up.' Helen obeyed, blinking rapidly at him as the sun became hurtful to her eyes. His hands touched her throat; he shook his head slightly and gave her an almost tender smile. 'I'd kiss you if we weren't being watched,' he said, and then, more briskly, 'Come, child, it's time for tea.'

The following day they went to Larnaca and, after parking the car, they strolled along the sea front, had refreshments at a little outdoor café under the palms and then went by car to the great salt lake, haunt of hundreds of flamingoes.

Helen was enchanted with them.

'Do they live here all the time?'

'No. We're lucky to see them; they'll be gone by the end of the month.'

'They're so beautiful!'

He smiled down at her.

'I knew you'd like this place. And now, would you care to go into the mountains?'

From the first it had been her pleasure he had considered. Something akin to affection entered her voice as she said,

'Yes, Leon, I'd like that,' and then, 'Are we far from Lefkara? I'd love to see the women making the lace. I'd like to buy some too, if I may?'

'Of course you may. You don't have to ask me that, Helen.'

They drove into the lovely mountain village where the world-famous 'Lefkaritika' lace was made. Leon bought her tablecloths and napkins, handkerchiefs by the dozen and an exquisitely-embroidered dress with an insert of the finest lace down the front and in the cuffs of the long full sleeves. Helen adored it, but gasped at the price.

'It's much too dear,' she protested as Leon held it up against her. 'And – and white might not suit me.'

'White does suit you.' Leon looked around.

'Madam may try it on.' The shopkeeper smiled and indicated a curtained recess at the back of the counter. 'It is just right for Madam, and as for the price—' She dismissed that minor detail with a flick of the hand. 'It is nothing.'

Nothing! Helen shook her head, but Leon told her to go and try on the dress. It fitted her beautifully. She stood before the mirror and caught her breath at her reflection.

'It's very lovely – but the price, Leon! It really is too expensive.'

'Nothing's too expensive for you, my dear,' and he added softly, as the woman went away to wrap up what they had bought, 'Didn't we say we'd be happy?'

'Yes, but—'

'And are you happy, Helen?' The merest tremor in his voice, and he watched her expression anxiously as he awaited her reply. A smile trembled on her lovely lips as she said, in a low and faintly husky tone,

'Yes, Leon. Yes, I am happy.'

# CHAPTER SIX

THE fleeting spring had blended almost imperceptibly into summer; the noon sun was high in the sky and visitors were flocking in their thousands to the coastal and hill resorts. But the lovely white house on the hillside high above Lapithos remained serenely unaffected by tourism, and as Helen lay on a deck chair in the garden she could not help admitting that, in many ways, she was lucky. A few months ago her life had been both lonely and dull, with no prospect other than that of working to keep herself. Fate played strange tricks, she mused, for if Brenda had not thought of her on learning of the plan to send Chippy and Fiona to their uncle, she would never even have set foot on this lovely island, much less have had the opportunity of making her home here. Lazily, she opened the book on her lap, but she made no attempt to read, and her eyes took on a brooding expression as she saw the gleaming black Mercedes winding its way up the hill. Life still held its problems, which was only to be expected, she thought, with a marriage that had taken place merely for necessity.

The holiday had eased the strain of their new relationship, but Helen could not forget that to Leon she was just another woman; that he made love to her without love. And with that knowledge ever present in her mind she could not forgive him for breaking the promise he initially made to her. She sighed, remembering her husband's agreeing with her that nothing was perfect. She and Leon had drifted into a way of life that was tolerable, and she supposed she should be thankful for that. It was preferable to the loathing she had at first experienced at his touch, the dread she had each time he came near to her.

She raised her head as he entered the paved garden, and managed a smile.

'Have you had a busy day?' she asked politely.

'Fairly. And you?'

'I think I'm becoming lazy. Araté does everything.'

'That's what she's paid for.' He stood looking at her, his dark eyes smiling. 'You've acquired a charming tan, my dear. Colour becomes you.'

'Thank you, Leon.' His compliments fell glibly, and often. If only they came from the heart, if only they were sincere. But they meant nothing; they had been paid to other women in the past – and would most likely be paid to women in the future ... when Leon eventually tired of his wife.

He fetched a chair and sat down opposite to her.

'We're visiting an aunt of mine this evening. She rang me today complaining that she hadn't yet met you.'

'Another aunt? You've never mentioned her.'

Leon smiled faintly at that.

'There are lots of things we still don't know about one another, aren't there?' And, when she merely nodded, 'How is it that natural conversation is so difficult between us, Helen?' The question surprised her. He appeared to be in one of those softer, almost gentle moods which always had the effect of producing in her an inexplicable feeling of guilt.

'I don't think we find conversation difficult.'

'I said natural conversation. Perhaps I should have said "confidences" are difficult between us.'

'It's understandable, I suppose – under the circumstances.'

Leon turned from her, his eyes narrowed against the sun as he glanced away, over the wooded slopes, to the smooth expanse of blue beyond.

'Why do you continue to harbour this resentment

103

against me?' The words came with difficulty, spoken with terrible bitterness. 'What's done is done.'

'Perhaps we shouldn't talk about it, Leon. We have before, you know, and the result is always strain between us. We must go through our lives together; let's try to do it peaceably, as far as possible.'

'You can resign yourself to this – for ever?' His dark head moved; the grey at his temples was turned to silver as the sun caught it. She thought, 'He looks older, much older, than when I first met him'.

'What else is there for us?'

'We haven't tried, Helen.' Turning to her he added, softly, "Don't you think we might try to – to—?'

'Are you expecting love from me?' A hint of bitterness had crept into her voice now and her eyes had darkened broodingly.

'No, Helen, I don't expect love . . . but it would be nice to feel your arms around me sometimes—' He broke off as she stiffened visibly and then continued, with a certain haste, as if he would have her forget that moment of weakness, of humility almost, 'No, I shall never expect love from you. You're not willing to give it – you told me that at the beginning, told me you'd never again allow your emotions to become involved – because of what some other man had done to you. That's right, isn't it?'

'Yes, yes, that's right.' She heard voices echoing on the hillside. Chippy and Fiona were playing with some of the children from the village. Why must they make such noise? Fiona's shrieks were louder than any. 'I said I'd never risk that sort of heartache again.'

'And you believe that's a reasonable attitude to adopt?'

'I shall never give another man an opportunity to hurt me. That's why I don't intend to fall in love again.'

'And yet you expect love from me?'

She glanced at him sharply, puzzled at his words.

'I've never expected love from you, Leon.'

'Then what is your complaint?' His eyes became hard and all the dark arrogance returned to his face. 'If you're not expecting love from me why the resentment?'

'You know why,' she answered as understanding dawned. 'It's not that you – you make love to me without love, but that you make love to me at all.'

He shrugged impatiently.

'You're both unrealistic and unreasonable.'

'Is it unreasonable to expect you to keep your promise? You made a proposition – asked me to marry you for the sake of the children, and I agreed, naturally believing you to be a man of your word.' He made no comment and she went on, 'Did you mean to keep your word – at the beginning, I mean?'

'I expect I did.'

'Then why did you change your mind?'

The echo of children's voices was the only sound as Leon hesitated, debating before he said,

'I'm going to be very outspoken, Helen, and you're not going to like it. When you came here you were drab and totally unattractive; you had nothing about you to arrest the attention of any man. The thought of – wanting you never entered my head.' He paused, watching the colour rise in her cheeks before continuing relentlessly, 'Although you would be my wife you were, as far as my feelings were concerned, nothing more than a servant, a nanny for the children. But I soon began to realize it was all a pose, that your drabness was intentional, and I gradually saw you as you could be—'

'Desirable?' she flashed, and his eyes glinted dangerously.

'If that is the word you care to use, yes. I was then curious to know what you were really like and indicated that I wished you to buy some clothes.'

'So that I could dress myself up and satisfy that curiosity? So that I could become a pretty plaything?' Suddenly she swallowed as she saw his expression. Stupid to go this far; she knew his fury of old.

'You readily dressed yourself up for someone else,' he snarled. 'For that damned Englishman!'

'I didn't—'

'You did!'

'All right, so I dressed myself up. You saw me and found me desirable. Was that any excuse for breaking your promise?'

'Forget the promise! It's become an obsession with you!'

'Forget . . . why should I? You made it and I expected you to keep it.'

'I've told you, you're being unrealistic. Do you think we could have gone on like that for forty years or more? Use your sense – you're not a child; you should have known!'

'Then so should you!'

'I realize that now—'

'Uncle Leon – Aunt Helen . . .!' The children's voices had been coming closer and now Fiona rushed into the garden, panting and ready to burst into tears. 'Don't let them get me!'

'Good gracious, child, what's the matter with you?' The change in Leon was miraculous. Taking the trembling child on his knee, he brought her head against him, stroking it soothingly. Fiona started to sob and he drew a handkerchief from his pocket. 'Here, this won't do—' He began to dry her eyes. 'What's it all about?'

'They – they—' The sobs still shook her, and she pressed close to her uncle as Chippy ran breathlessly into the garden, closely followed by two other boys of about his age. They were all waving sticks and screaming wildly, but they stopped dead on seeing Fiona on Leon's knee.

'Oh,' said Chippy, going rather pale.

Leon looked up, glancing from his nephew to his two young companions and then bringing his gaze back to settle on the stick in Chippy's hand.

'What are you supposed to be doing?' Even Helen found herself trembling at his tone, and her heartbeats quickened, for she was sure Chippy was in for real trouble.

'We're playing prisons,' Chippy supplied reluctantly.

'Prisons?'

'They had me locked up – in the old Turkish house down in the woods,' sobbed Fiona, 'and they said they'd leave me there for ever!'

'We didn't mean it,' put in Chippy urgently. 'You know we didn't.'

'We did!' Andreas cast a derisive glance in Fiona's direction. 'She's only a girl.'

'We didn't mean it,' said Alex, more observant than his young friend. 'We wouldn't have left her there, Mr. Petrou, honest.'

Leon transferred his gaze, examining the two boys in turn.

'Take yourselves off,' he said, very quietly. 'I shall see your fathers in the morning.'

'Oh, Mr. Petrou—'

'I said go home!'

Andreas obeyed, sulkily, but Alex remained where he was, his brown face troubled.

'Father will beat me—'

'You should have thought about that earlier. Little girls are to be taken care of, not chased with sticks. I'm surprised at you, Alex, and I hope the beating will do you good. Now do as I say and go home.'

'Yes, Mr. Petrou.' He took a few flagging steps towards the path, then turned. 'I'm sorry, Fiona. I won't ever chase you again.' He swallowed hard, cast an unhappy glance at Helen, and then went off, his footsteps still flagging. Helen determined to put in a good word for Alex – later, when her husband was in a more receptive mood.

Fiona was still crying and Helen said,

'Let me take her, Leon.' He put her down, and she went to Helen. She was still trembling and Leon's dark eyes were hard and angry as, getting to his feet, he beckoned Chippy to come to him. The child obeyed reluctantly; his head was jerked up as his uncle gripped his chin.

'Now, young man, I'll have a full explanation. What do you mean by locking your sister up in that house?'

'How could they lock her up?' asked Helen, puzzled. The old Turkish house was practically in ruins. It had been empty for over thirty years. 'There are no windows in it.'

'That's h-how I g-got out,' sobbed Fiona. 'I had to climb up and – and I t-tore my dress. And then I ran and they chased me.' She'd had a bad fright, there was no doubt of that, and Helen was not surprised when Leon grasped Chippy by the shoulders and shook him hard.

'Answer me,' he ordered, unmoved by the sudden brightness of his nephew's eyes. 'Answer me at once!'

'We were only playing, Uncle Leon, truly. Andreas said let's play at prisons, and there was no one else to lock up – well, the boys didn't want to be locked up.'

'And so you seized your sister, did you?' His voice was like thunder. Chippy nodded dumbly and cast an appealing glance at Helen.

'I still don't see how they locked her up?' she persisted, frowning. 'There's no door on that house.'

'It was in the p-part where they used to k-keep the cows and things.'

'I'm waiting, Chippy,' Leon snapped, ignoring both Helen's remarks and Fiona's explanation. 'I want to know exactly what happened!'

'We put her in,' Chippy began, in trembling tones. 'And then we closed those gates across the doorway—'

'Gates?'

'Oh, yes,' Helen said, tightening her hold comfortably as Fiona shuddered at the recollection. 'There are some heavy gates – but they're rusty and haven't been closed for years, by the look of them—'

'You put your sister in there and then closed the gates?' Leon shook him again and Chippy started to cry.

'Leon, don't—'

'I'll handle this!' His jaw was tight, his brow black with fury. 'How did you manage to close those gates?'

'Alex and I did it – with another boy. He ran off when Fiona began to scream.'

'What was Andreas doing?'

'He was guarding me.' Fiona sat up and glanced balefully at her brother. 'I wanted Chippy to help me, but he didn't – he let Andreas stand there, with a stick, in case I ran away—'

'You were the prisoner, Fiona, and you said at first you didn't mind.' He looked at his sister. 'The stick wasn't to hit you with. It was supposed to be a gun – you know that. You said you didn't mind,' he repeated, a note of indignation creeping into his voice.

'I didn't think you were going to shut the gates—' She turned to Leon and the tears streamed down her face again. 'Andreas said the gates were magic and that once you closed them nobody could open them again, and that I'd never get out, never!' She was becoming hysterical, and Leon told Helen to take her inside and give her a sedative.

'But Chippy . . .?' Helen glanced appealingly at her husband, even though she had to admit Chippy deserved to be severely punished. 'What are you going to do?'

'I think,' he replied, reaching down to take the stick from Chippy's hand, 'that a taste of this on his legs won't do him any harm.'

'Oh, no!' Helen stood up, her face very pale. Fiona still clung to her, but she was looking up at her uncle. 'Not that, Leon,' begged Helen, shaking her head. 'He'll remember it for the rest of his life – and he'll always feel resentful.'

Her words had an odd effect on Leon. He stared at her with a hint of bewilderment in his eyes as he said, almost forgetting the presence of the children,

'You sound as if your concern is with me rather than the child.'

'It is,' she confessed, her eyes never wavering from his face. 'Don't, Leon – *please!*'

'The idea of Chippy's harbouring resentment against me troubles you?'

She knew the reason for his puzzlement, but she had to tell the truth.

'Yes, Leon, it does trouble me. Chippy has a great admiration and respect for you. I wouldn't like his opinion of you to change.'

Her husband shook his head and a sigh left his lips.

'You're a strange girl, Helen. I can't understand you at all.' He held her gaze, and an odd expression entered his eyes. Did he read her thoughts? Was he aware that she could not understand herself?

'Chippy?' she said again, managing to escape her husband's penetrating gaze at last.

'You need have no fear; I shall not beat him.'

Later, as she sat beside Fiona's bed, waiting for the drooping lids to close finally in sleep, Helen went over the scene again. The way Leon had taken Fiona on his knee, soothing her and gently drying her tears; the way he had told Alex that little girls should be cared for. With a flash of memory Helen recalled her early reading of Leon's character, reaching the conclusion that he was a man of dual personality.

Harsh and tender, arrogant and humble, pleading and demanding ... she had seen him in so many changing moods. Which was the real Leon? she wondered. How would she ever find out? She shrugged, frowning, and leant forward to bring up the sheet which Fiona had disarranged. Why should she care which was the real Leon? She was not interested, and yet. . . . Again a frown creased her brow. No use denying it, she could not remain totally insensitive to her husband, for in any mood his influence could be felt.

'Is Uncle Leon going to be very cross with Chippy?' Fiona murmured sleepily, trying to keep her eyes open. It was the third time she had asked the question.

'Just you go to sleep, darling, and never mind about Chippy—'

'But—'

'Close your eyes, dear.'

'I don't want Chippy to be punished.'

'I'm afraid he'll have to be.'

'Can't you tell Uncle Leon not to?'

'Uncle Leon will do what he thinks is right.'

Fiona became silent, and gradually drifted into sleep. Quietly Helen slipped away. Leon was alone on the verandah and she went out to him there.

'Where's Chippy?'

'In his room. He goes there each day on coming from school; you will see to that.'

'How long for?'

'Until I decide he has learned his lesson. His pocket money, too, will be stopped.' Rising, he gave her his chair, reaching for another one for himself. 'I can't understand the boy. Where does he get these ideas?'

'The village boys apparently don't think much of females. No doubt they follow the example of their fathers.'

'Was that necessary?' he asked coldly, and she lowered her head under the rebuke.

'I'll go and help Araté with the meal,' she said, getting up. 'What time are we going out?'

'As soon as we've dined. Perhaps we could have the meal a little earlier?'

'Yes, I expect so.' She turned into the sitting-room, but he called her back.

'Helen. . . .'

'Yes?'

'The picture? Have you started it yet?'

'Only just; I can't show it to you until—'

'Fetch it.'

'You won't like it – not until I've done more.'

'Let me see it.'

Resignedly she shrugged and a few moments later returned with the canvas. She blushed self-consciously as she handed it to him.

'I'm not very good, Leon – I told you I wasn't.' Embarrassed, she looked away, her eyes scanning the little wooded rise that formed the outer edge of the garden. Walnut trees were growing there and palms. Bananas grew there too, and figs; in fact, every kind of tree seemed to flourish on that rise. Below and nearer to, jacarandas splashed their vivid blue against the snow-white supports of the archway leading to the rose garden. Everywhere there was colour. Mimosa, hibiscus, oleander ... such lovely names—

'What gave you the idea of painting the old mill?' Her husband's soft and curious tones intruded into her thoughts and she turned around, looking down at him as he held the canvas in his hands, regarding it inscrutably.

'It has a strange attraction for me,' she confessed. 'It's in such an enchanting spot, with the water gushing out from the hillside – it's lovely to see water like that here.

In England these natural springs are everywhere, but here I haven't seen many at all.'

'The old mill. . . .' His thoughts were no longer with her; his dark eyes held an expression half dreamy and half sad. He looked so terribly alone. For some inexplicable reason Helen caught her breath. This was her husband in one of his childlike moods. It was ridiculous, but she had an almost irresistible desire to put her arms around him. . . . Something in her heart felt strange. How odd that, only a short while back, he had said, with an unmistakable hint of sadness in his voice, that he would like to feel her arms around him sometimes. And she had stiffened, not trying to hide her feelings. But yet . . . it was not revulsion that caused her to stiffen, for that she had not felt since their little holiday. Why, then, had she stiffened? Suddenly she knew she had not actually stiffened at all; the jerk of her body had been a gesture of hauteur . . . and it was merely to cover up that feeling of remorse which persistently stole over her when she and Leon had these arguments. Why should she feel guilty? Indignation sparkled in her eyes as she asked herself the question. She was entirely blameless. Leon was to blame for everything and he it should be who was troubled by a feeling of remorse. He was still lost in thought and, loth to break in on his reverie, she stood there waiting, and watching his expression change as his eyes focused on the canvas again. 'This was my grandfather's home.' He smiled up at her, tapping the painting with his finger. 'There were lots of grandchildren then, but we're scattered now, for many of them have left the island to find work elsewhere. We used to gather at the mill for Christmas, and at Easter – in fact, at all the festive and holiday times.' He paused, then added, 'The mill belongs to me—'

'To you? I didn't know, Leon; you didn't tell me.'

'I wasn't aware you'd found it. Obviously you've been

rambling round in your spare time.'

'I discovered it quite by accident, when I was out walking with the children. We wandered down this rough and rocky track "exploring", the children said, and suddenly, there it was – a lovely picture, with the water glistening in the sun as it bounded down from the cleft in the rocks.'

'You put it very prettily,' he commented, amusement in his smile. Helen flushed and her lovely mouth curved in response. Leon's eyes darkened and then his lids came down, masking his expression. Did she misjudge him? she wondered, for it seemed to Helen that every time he looked at her there was desire in his eyes.

'It's so sad that it's now in ruins, and all overgrown. Can't anything be done with it?'

'As a matter of fact, I'm selling it. And it's odd that you should have chosen to paint it because Phil was saying recently that we ought to have some record of it, as it is, before its character is lost in the renovations.'

'There are to be renovations?'

'The man who's buying it is a wealthy financier from your country. He intends to keep as much as possible, I believe, but naturally he'll have to make extensive alterations to the place.'

'He'll take away most of the character, you think?' Regret clouded her eyes. She must be a little peculiar, she thought, for renovations of this kind always made her feel sad.

'I'm sure he'll convert it into a charming property. Far better to let someone have the benefit, not only of the place itself, but of the view. It happens to be one of the best in Lapithos.'

'Yes. The sea and the mountains – just like this.' She spoke musingly, an almost tender light in her eyes, and she scarcely realized her whispered words were audible as she added, 'What more could one want?'

A deep sigh answered her and she glanced swiftly at

him. His eyes were faintly bitter, but his voice assumed a lightness as he said,

'I shall like your painting, my dear, but I knew I should.' He held it out to her and she took it from him, experiencing pleasure that he was not disappointed in her work.

Leon's Aunt Chrisoula lived alone in a massive Greek-style house. It had been built by her father sixty years ago when his children numbered sixteen. Some had since died and the others were either married or living elsewhere.

'About time,' she grumbled on opening the door. She examined Helen from head to foot before stepping back to allow her and Leon to enter. 'I was beginning to feel I had the plague, or something!'

Leon merely laughed and, once inside, he turned to introduce his wife.

'English, eh?' His aunt shrugged. 'Oh, well, I expect you know what you're doing.'

'It's already done, Aunt Chrisoula.' The cynical note apparently escaped the old woman, but a soft flush touched Helen's cheeks on hearing it. 'We're an old married couple by now.' Taking Helen's arm, he propelled her gently into the sitting-room, following in the wake of his aunt. 'It's time you did something about getting rid of this old house.'

'Might as well die here now. Sit down on the couch – move the cats, Helen, they think they own the place.'

'Sit here.' Leon grinned and gave her a chair that appeared to be reasonably clean. 'What do you want all these cats for, anyway?' he called over his shoulder, for his aunt had gone off into the kitchen.

'All strays – they're everywhere. Dogs, too, but I can't be taking them in all the time. Besides, they bark, and I'm too old for that sort of noise.' Her English was far from perfect, but Helen had no difficulty in understanding it.

She was looking around her and uttering little gasps under her breath.

'This is nothing,' Leon whispered. 'Wait till she shows you over the house.'

The room was more like a huge barn, complete with flagstone floor and worm-eaten beams supporting the walls and ceiling. There were stuffed birds perched on twigs or in cages. Others were in glass domes and looking as if the moths had fed on their feathers for years. Under glass domes too were ornaments and decorations from wedding-cakes, and on the wood-lined walls were literally dozens of photographs – obviously of members of Aunt Chrisoula's family. Cats occupied every seat other than those on which Helen and Leon were sitting, and several others were stretched out on the rug by the empty fire-place.

Presently Aunt Chrisoula returned with a tray on which were three glasses of water and three cut-glass plates each containing a peculiar-looking black object about the size of a small egg. These were on the end of long silver forks, and from them dripped a thick black syrup which settled in little pools on the plates. Helen eyed them suspiciously and felt rather sick. A tiny shake of her head indicated to Leon that she did not want one, and a firm inclination of *his* head told her that she must not refuse.

The tray was in front of her; she had no idea what to do and during her brief hesitation some conversation in Greek began to take place between Leon and his aunt.

'No, not walnuts. . . .' Aunt Chrisoula's brow was furrowed. 'Come, child.'

'Thank you.' Helen picked up one of the plates, but Leon took it from her and returned it to the tray.

'Take hold of the glass,' he said, handing it to her. 'Now, take up the fork. You dip the—?' His brow furrowed and he spoke again in Greek to his aunt. 'Ah,

Brazil nuts—'

'Brazil nuts?' ejaculated Helen unbelievingly. 'This size – and colour?'

'Take up the nut and, each time you have a bite, you dip the nut in the water.'

'Do I?' She eyed the glass, and the revolting object stuck on the end of her fork. With stoic perseverence she had forced herself to become used to the food here, but never had she been faced with anything so objectionable as this.

'It's the colour,' she complained. 'Must I, Leon?'

'Taste it,' he commanded, and reluctantly she did as she was told. Then to her husband's amusement and satisfaction her eyes widened.

'O–oh. . . . It's delicious!'

'I haven't seen these for years,' Leon said, biting into the sweetmeat and savouring its taste for a moment before congratulating his aunt on her expert treatment of the nuts. 'Helen, dip it in your glass.' She obeyed, but wanted to know the reason for doing this. 'It's the correct way to eat these nuts. The syrup keeps oozing out and you wash it away in the water.'

'They're so big. I can't believe this is a Brazil nut.'

'They swell with the treatment,' he informed her. 'Also, the kernel is here, too.'

After the sweetmeats came drinks; this time Helen had a choice, and as always, she drank orange juice.

'I'll take you over the house.' Aunt Chrisoula offered when they had finished, and Leon cast a glance at Helen and grinned.

'You'll never believe you're in a house,' he warned. 'It's vast.'

Not only was it vast, but it was in a shocking state of disrepair. They went into one room after another, each appearing more neglected than the last. There were more birds, and also small animals, stuffed and thick with dust.

In one massive glass case a most gory tableau was displayed. Birds of prey, holding their victims with one taloned claw and tearing at the flesh with their beaks. Everywhere there were icons, and in front of many of them were tiny red lights, produced by minute electric bulbs. The wires connecting these bulbs were sometimes trailing across the floor, sometimes in a tangled mass coming down the wall from the plug.

'These are genuine,' Leon whispered. 'Worth a fortune.'

'The icons, you mean?'

He nodded. His aunt looked questioningly at him and spoke to him in Greek.

'I'm telling Helen your icons are extremely valuable,' he said in slow and emphasized tones.

'No fakes here,' she said, stopping to move one of the lights into the centre of the picture. 'Very old – yes, very old.' She stopped again to straighten up the painting of St. Nicholas which had slipped and was leaning against another of the icons. 'I kiss them every night,' she said, and Helen blinked.

'You kiss them . . . ? Every one?'

'Every one.' She preceded them across a wide landing into yet another bedroom. Helen had lost count of the rooms and she wondered how an old lady like this could bear to live in such a place.

'I'd be so terrified,' she whispered to Leon. 'I couldn't live in a house like this.'

'Aunt Chrisoula's been here all her life, remember. She's used to it.'

'But all alone. And you say these icons are very valuable. She could be attacked.'

'Attacked?' He looked amazed. 'We never have that sort of violence here.'

'Never?' It was Helen's turn now to look amazed. 'No burglaries?'

'Very, very seldom. No, Helen, this is the difference

between contentment and avarice. Here, people are content. I expect it's something to do with the climate. Sunshine makes you happy.' He smiled at her, and even though he himself appeared quite content and happy there was a hint of yearning in his manner which caused her once again to know that feeling of remorse. But stronger by far was the sensation of unrest; there was a void within her too for which she could not account. Leon's hand dropped on to her shoulder as he guided her towards the bedroom in which his aunt was waiting. Helen could not suppress a shudder at the coldness of the room and she felt his fingers move caressingly, then draw her close to him. His touch was so very gentle . . . could it be that he cared a little? – that he had some small affection for her? Or was it that he just had to touch her? Helen swallowed hard, releasing the tightness of emotion in her throat. Supposing he did care a little – could she care, too? She thought of Gregory and the way he had let her down. So unsuspecting she had been, so blindly trusting. No, she would never allow herself to care again. She had made a vow never to trust another man, never to leave herself open to be hurt and duped a second time.

'It was a fine house when Father built it,' Aunt Chrisoula was saying, 'but it's rather neglected now, for I can't get round it the same as I used to. I suppose I should sell it, as you say, Leon, but I think I'm too old to start moving now.'

'Nonsense. Let me sell it for you.'

'Can you get me a good price?'

'Very. The position's perfect.' He turned to Helen. 'We must come again in the daylight. Aunt Chrisoula has lovely grounds here – with every kind of tree and shrub you can mention, to say nothing of the flowers. She spends all her time outside, so naturally the house is neglected.'

'What are you saying, Leon? I wish you'd either talk in

your own language or talk more slowly.'

'Sorry, Aunt Chrisoula, but Helen doesn't know Greek. I was trying to describe the gardens to her.'

'The gardens, yes.' The old woman pointed a thin white finger at the shutters. 'Lovely views, too, lovely.'

Helen had to smile, for she suspected that the shutters were scarcely ever opened.

'Are you going to think about it?' Leon asked as they came downstairs and went back into the sitting-room.

'Think about it?' She stared at him absently.

'Selling the house?'

'Where would I go?'

'I'd find you something small and easy to run.'

'Cheap?'

His mouth curved in amusement.

'You're just like everyone else,' he laughed. 'You want top price for your own house, but you hope to buy cheaply.'

'What do you say?'

Leon obligingly repeated it and she agreed that that was what she wanted.

'I'll see what I can do.'

'Well . . . no – er – perhaps I'd better wait a while.'

'Always we have this,' he told Helen. 'Every time I come Aunt Chrisoula considers selling the house, and always she changes her mind.'

'It's the cats. What would I do with them?'

'I've told you often enough what to do with them.'

'You're heartless and cruel! Don't you find him so, Helen?'

A hint of colour fused Helen's cheeks, but she remained silent. Leon regarded her flushed countenance with a sort of sardonic amusement.

'Well, my dear, aren't you going to answer Aunt Chrisoula?'

'No need to. I'm sure you bully the poor girl shamefully.' She picked up one of the cats and placed it on her knee. 'How do you like Leon's beautiful house?'

'Very much,' returned Helen enthusiastically. 'I've never seen anything quite like it.'

'No. It's just about the nicest house around these parts.' She paused and frowned, and then regarded Leon for a moment.

'Perhaps I will think about selling this place. Yes, you can look out for a bungalow for me.'

'Do you really mean that?'

'Yes, I do. I can find room for the cats.'

They talked a little while longer and then Leon said they must go.

'Araté doesn't like to stay too late,' he explained. 'So we must get back. How about paying us a visit?' he added, rising.

'Would be nice – and I haven't seen those children. You'll have to come and fetch me; my old legs won't get me very far.'

'I'll come and fetch you.' It was arranged that she should come over the following Sunday and have lunch with them. Then Leon would take her home later in the afternoon.

'Don't forget to look for that bungalow,' she reminded him as he was about to drive away.

'I think I know someone who might have just the thing for Aunt Chrisoula,' Leon said as they were driving home along the coast road. 'I'm pleased that she's at last considering selling that old house.'

'It's far too big for her,' Helen agreed. 'Just imagine occupying two or three rooms, and being surrounded by all those others – so bare and cold. It can't be very pleasant for her.'

'I agree. Well, we must see what we can do. As I've said, I know someone who might have the very thing for her.'

# CHAPTER SEVEN

So intent was she on her work that Helen did not realize she was being watched until she heard her husband's voice behind her. It was raised above the noise of the water cascading down into the pool by the side of the mill. She turned, faintly embarrassed.

'Nearly finished?' His dark eyes were fixed admiringly on the canvas. 'How quick you've been!'

'It was the encouragement,' she smiled, stepping back in order to survey her work from a distance. 'How did you know I was here?'

'Araté told me.'

'You're home early.'

'It was becoming too hot in the office.' The afternoon was not particularly hot. This was the third day running that he had come home early. Was it possible that he wanted to be with her? Hastily dismissing the idea, she gave her full attention to the painting. Her smile faded and a slight frown creased her brow.

'I haven't quite enough shading below that arch.'

'The encouragement,' Leon said, returning to her earlier remark. 'You sound as if you've never before received encouragement?' She did not reply and he turned her round to face him. 'Is that why you haven't done any before? – why you had nothing to show me when I asked to see some of your work?'

Although she nodded she still did not speak. Gregory had disparaged her work, and she had lost confidence in herself. But that was all in the past; she had no wish to tell Leon about it. But he insisted and at last she said,

'Gregory didn't like my style – he didn't think anyone would buy my paintings.'

'Did you want to sell them?'

She considered this.

'It wasn't the money, but it would have been nice to think someone would buy them. Phil was saying that with artists it's not the money as much as the satisfaction that matters. And satisfaction comes only when your work is appreciated.'

'Very true. . . .' He became thoughtful for a while. 'Our local artists are having an exhibition of their work – in Nicosia. I shall include yours.'

'Oh, will you?' Her blue eyes shone, but after a moment the light went out of them as she said, disappointment creeping into her voice, 'It won't be good enough—' She shook her head again, vigorously. 'No, it really won't, Leon.'

'I told you before that I'd be the judge. It's going in the exhibition.' The confidence in his voice – and the unmistakable hint of pride in his eyes!

'It's kind of you to encourage me,' she said impulsively. 'I do appreciate it.' Could words convey just how deep her appreciation went? The desire to paint had always been strong within her, and at one time she had considered her work to be at least passable; but Gregory had convinced her that she was no good at all, and consequently she had become discouraged. Now she would begin once more to indulge in her hobby, to derive pleasure from it – and from any praise her husband might give to her.

'I consider your work to be good, so naturally I must encourage you.' His voice was caressingly soft and without warning happiness flooded over her. What was happening? Was it only a few days since she had asked herself 'could she care?' Now she was struggling to prevent herself from caring. And she knew her struggles would prove to be in vain. That broken promise, Leon's unkindness on the night she had been out with Robert, the disunion

123

between them – all these had been gradually fading during these past few days; they no longer seemed important. What was important was that Leon could look at her like this, could speak to her with softness in his voice, could touch her with such gentleness.

'I must go back,' she said, profoundly aware of the warmth of his hands on her arms. 'The children will be home from school already.'

'Araté is there.' But he took the canvas from her as she lifted it off the easel. 'Where did you say you leave these?'

'In that little outhouse. I've cleaned it and Nikos came along and fixed the door.'

'Will it be all right?' Leon frowned as he glanced at the tiny stone building, and then, decisively, 'I'll put the easel in there, but we'll take the painting back to the house.'

Did he really think such a lot about it? Watching him as he carried the easel over to the outhouse, Helen experienced again that little access of happiness, and her eyes were glowing as, having secured the door, he walked back with the canvas in his hand.

He had the car at the end of the lane and within minutes they were home. Chippy's punishment still continued and Fiona was in the garden with the dog. Hearing the car in the drive, she ran to it. She looked far from happy, and Helen believed she suffered as much as her brother by the separation.

'Can't Chippy leave his room now?' Helen begged, a few moments later when they were sitting out under the trees. 'It's three days, Leon, and that's a long time.'

'Has he learned his lesson, do you think?'

'He knows now how wrong it was. I'm sure he'll take good care of Fiona in future.'

Rather to Helen's surprise Leon relented, though he sternly lectured Chippy when he came out to them in the garden.

'I think you're right,' he observed, watching Chippy with Fiona as they played together later in the afternoon. 'He'll not do anything like that again.'

Eventually the children left the garden and wandered out on to the hillside. Their voices gradually died away and a deep silence settled over the garden. Apart from the gentle motion of the palms and the flutter of wings in the flower-strewn borders, nothing stirred. Helen leant back in her chair and stole a sideways glance at her husband. His face was in the shadows, but now and then a glint of sunshine would penetrate the thick foliage above him and the sprinklings of grey in his hair would be thrown into relief. His eyes were closed and he appeared to be enveloped in a deep peace. But every now and then his lips would move slightly and the impression was instantly dispelled. What were his thoughts and feelings? In the beginning she had concluded that there was no depth to his emotions, but recently she had begun to have doubts. She withdrew her gaze, closing her own eyes as she tried to visualize the future now that she had accepted the fact that her heart was touched. If only it were possible that Leon could care, then she could see a happiness that surpassed anything she had ever known . . . but if Leon did not care. . . . Then there was nothing, except perhaps disillusionment a second time. If all she had heard about the Cypriot temperament were true, then she was in a most precarious position, for undoubtedly there would come a time when he would tire of her.

The silence was broken by the laughter of several children playing in the woods below; Leon opened his eyes and the hint of a frown touched his dark forehead.

'They're with those boys from the village.' He cocked an ear and listened. 'They sound as if they're at the old Turkish house again.' Although he did not move for a while he was restless and eventually he rose from his chair. 'Come,' he invited, extending a hand to her, 'we'll go down and see what's going on.' His concern for Fiona was very real, and Helen reflected on Brenda's assertion that he had no liking for children and wondered how the idea had originated. Strict and stern he might be, but it was far from true that he disliked children.

As he had suspected, Fiona and Chippy were with Alex and Andreas, and they were all playing in the Turkish house. Chippy saw them first and ran to them.

'We're not playing prisons,' he informed Leon hastily. 'We're playing Red Indians.'

'I'm an Indian, too,' put in Fiona. 'I'll shoot you with my arrow!'

'You'd shoot your uncle?' Helen withdrew her hand from his and walked over to examine a pretty little flower growing in the stonework of the building.

'No, I wouldn't—' Fiona ran to her uncle and flung her arms around his legs. 'I love him too much.'

Slowly Helen turned; Leon was staring down at the animated little face of his niece and his expression was tender. And then he looked up, and across at Helen. She heard him saying, 'It would be nice to feel your arms round me sometimes' and as her eyes looked into his the last of her doubts fled away.

He cared. He would never let her down.

'I think I'll have this place demolished,' he decided, a little while later as he and Helen were examining the deep cracks in the structure. 'It's far from safe, and there's nothing pretty about it, either.'

'Is it yours?' asked Helen in surprise, and Leon nodded.

'Something else I inherited. I suppose the sensible thing is to sell this, too, but it could be that our view would be affected – if someone were to build on stilts, which is very probable. No, I'll have it pulled down.' The gates were still closed and he opened them. Helen stepped inside and Fiona shouted to her uncle not to close them on her.

'I told you,' she added, running up to him, 'if you shut them when there's anyone inside they won't open again – because they're magic.'

'You believe anything,' said Alex, laughing. 'It's not true; they're not magic at all.'

'Well, Andreas said they were, and that's why I was frightened. You said the one inside would never, never escape.' Teasingly, Leon made to close them, but Fiona tugged at his hand. 'No!'

'Don't upset her.' Helen came out of the building and Fiona's face cleared. 'I should have thought you'd have more sense than to take notice of these stupid boys,' she said, laughing, and then, 'It's time you came home, anyway. You must be getting hungry.'

They all walked back together and, later, when the children were in bed and Helen and Leon were having dinner, Leon brought up the question of the holiday he had previously mentioned.

'If we went to Paphos we could go and see Mother – we can't stay there because she hasn't the room – and I could have a look at that land I'm thinking of buying.'

Feeling actually excited at the prospect, Helen readily entered into discussion about the projected holiday, and it was decided they would take it in three weeks' time, when the children were on holiday from school.

'I shall have to do some shopping,' she said. 'The children will need a few new things. I'll do it the next time I go to see Trudy.'

Meanwhile, Aunt Chrisoula visited them as arranged. Helen wore the dress Leon had bought her; she came out of the bedroom into the sitting-room, an unaccountable shyness descending on her as she watched his changing expression. He stared at her in silent admiration for some moments before he said,

'My beautiful wife. . . .' And in a little while he smiled,

127

a smile of tender amusement. 'Dare I hold such a lovely creature?'

For answer she went to him. She put her arms around him and lifted her face for his kiss.

Ten minutes later he said,

'I must go and fetch Aunt Chrisoula. I shan't be long.'

No sooner had he arrived back with the old lady than another car pulled up in the drive. Asmena and Vasilios got out and were cordially greeted by their nephew.

'You'll stay for lunch?' He glanced at Helen, a question in his eyes. She nodded. No Cypriot house was without its well-stocked larder.

'No, Leon, we'll not trouble you.' Asmena smiled down at Fiona as the child came running up to her. 'We're just going out for a little drive.'

'Of course you must stay,' Helen interposed. 'Aunt Chrisoula is here.'

'Here? You've managed to get her out? I congratulate you; she always refuses our invitations.' She looked at her husband; he was leaning against the car, idly twirling his string of worry beads. An involuntary frown appeared on Helen's brow; her husband saw it and amusement lit his eyes. 'Shall we stay?' Asmona asked, and Vasilios merely nodded.

At first the children were shy of Aunt Chrisoula – in fact, they were a trifle scared of her, for she did look rather forbidding, clad from head to foot in black. Her dark face was wrinkled and her hands were thin and gnarled. She had never been married, and Helen expected her to have little patience with the children, but the opposite was the case. Quickly losing their fear, Chippy and Fiona were soon chatting away to her, and it was clear that she was really enjoying the break that this outing was giving her. Asmena and Vasilios were pleased to see her and when Leon informed them of Aunt Chrisoula's intention of selling her house they were in complete agreement with this decision she had so unexpectedly made.

'What you want is a nice, small bungalow,' stated Asmena. 'One like ours would suit you.'

'Too expensive. I want a smaller property than that. Leon will find me one.'

Vasilios looked at his nephew in some surprise.

'You don't deal in small properties, do you?' he asked, and Leon shook his head.

'I know someone who does, though,' he added. 'I'm sure we shall find exactly what Aunt Chrisoula requires.'

After lunch the children went off to play again and coffee was brought into the sitting-room. Leon had closed the shutters and the room was lighted by electricity.

'Can't we have the shutters open?' Helen looked up at Leon in some surprise. Hitherto he had always agreed with her that it was a pity to shut out the sun. 'It seems ridiculous to have to sit in artificial light when it isn't necessary.'

'Just for now, darling. Aunt Chrisoula will feel much more at home.'

'Of course.' Colour swept up into her face at the endearment. She was not yet used to it – but then it was only two days since she had first let Leon feel her arms around him.

Trudy noticed the change in her when next Helen paid a visit to the flat.

'What's happened to you?' Trudy stared at her glowing face unbelievingly. 'You look as if you've come into a fortune.'

'Perhaps I have.' And, after a small pause, 'Do I look so different?'

'I hardly know you,' Trudy laughed, and added teasingly,

'After all your determination never to fall in love – how did it happen?' They both laughed then, for there was no answer to Trudy's question.

'Leon's told me to ask you over to see us,' Helen said as they sat in Trudy's blue and white kitchen having a snack before going into the town. 'We want you to come to dinner. But we're going away for a few days, so we'll fix on a date when we come back.'

'A honeymoon?'

Helen looked out into the tree-lined road and thought of the few days she and Leon had spent in Famagusta. That, she supposed, was when it had all really begun.

'No; the children are coming with us.'

'Oh. . . .' Trudy seemed disappointed. 'You're landed with those two kids. Don't you mind?'

'I love them,' Helen returned swiftly. 'We both do.' Her eyes returned to the road. Among the shiny leaves of the trees opposite, oranges and lemons and mandarins were appearing, small and very green. 'They've missed a lot, but we're making it up to them now.'

'I have ever such a lot of shopping to do,' Helen apologized when eventually they arrived in the town, having come from the flat by bus. 'For the children, mainly, but I need a couple of dresses for myself.'

Their shopping finished, the two girls went to their favourite café and, having suffered the usual stares from the eyes of every man present, they managed to take their refreshments in reasonable comfort.

It was only four o'clock when they came out of the café and Helen decided not to return to the flat and wait for Theo to come and fetch her, but to make her own way to her husband's office.

'As you wish,' said Trudy. 'I can show you where to get the bus.'

Their way back took them past a row of souvenir shops and on glancing in one of the windows Helen uttered a little exclamation and stopped.

'One of Robert's paintings.' She pointed it out to her friend. 'It's good, don't you think?'

'Hmm ... yes, I like it— Oh, how remiss of me,' she added contritely. 'I never asked how your picture has been received.'

Flushing, Helen said that it had been very well received and she had been asked to paint scenes on two of the walls of a large new villa which was being built by an Englishman who was settling in Cyprus on his retirement in a few months' time.

'He liked Robert's work, too, and he's doing some paintings in the dining-room.'

'In the same house?' And when Helen nodded, 'Where is this house? It sounds as if it's going to be fabulous.'

'In Kyrenia ... well, just outside, but not very far from Lapithos, only about seven miles or so.'

'How are you going to get there?'

'On the bus; it won't be any trouble.'

'How does Leon take to the idea?' Trudy asked, and there was a slight pause before Helen replied,

'He's pleased, for me. He knows I enjoy painting.' He'd been far from pleased, though, on learning that Robert would also be painting at the house. But he had not made an issue of it and, to Helen's intense relief, had allowed the matter to drop.

'Where is your painting now?'

'Leon has it in his office— Well, I expect it's up by this time.' The pleasure in her eyes and voice brought a swift smile to her friend's lips.

'He must be in love – wanting your picture before him all day long!'

They had moved on and were now standing at the bus stop. It soon came and Trudy waved goodbye as Helen boarded it, her arms full of parcels.

'Have a nice time,' Trudy called. 'See you when you come back!'

It was only a short distance to the office and as Helen entered her husband glanced up at the clock.

'Is something wrong? Theo was coming for you in about half an hour.'

'I thought I'd come straight on here after we'd done our shopping.' She dropped her parcels on to a chair and sat down on another. Leon smiled and pushed the bell on his desk.

'I'll get you a drink; you look hot. Why did you carry all those parcels? They could have been sent.'

'They're not all that heavy.' She was looking around; Leon had not yet hung her picture. He must have been too busy. Where was it? she wondered. It would not fit in any of the drawers – and it was nowhere to be seen.

Theo came in with coffee for Leon and orange for Helen.

'I think I can finish now,' Leon said, glancing swiftly over the papers before him. 'Yes, drink up and we'll go.'

Should she mention the picture? But no; she felt that was not quite the right thing to do, and instead, she asked him if he were sure she had not inconvenienced him by coming early.

'There's no need for you to leave your work,' she added, looking at him anxiously. 'I don't mind waiting.'

'No, dear, we'll go.' He gathered up the parcels and carried them out to the car. 'Did you get everything you wanted?'

'Yes; and I bought swimming trunks for the children. Will we be going in the sea?'

'Of course. There's a beautiful beach to the west of Paphos. We must go there.'

The children were bubbling over with excitement, and

Helen herself was affected by it. She had never looked forward so much to anything in her life, and even though the preparation naturally produced extra work, every little chore was a pleasure.

'When will it come?' Fiona could scarcely contain her impatience. 'I wish it was Friday; I can't wait.'

'You'll have to, I'm afraid,' was her uncle's calm response. 'You have two more days at school first, and then we shall be on our way.'

'How long are we going for?'

'About a week.'

'A whole week?'

'If you behave, that is.'

'We'll be good, won't we, Fiona?'

'I'm always good,' she retorted. 'It's you what's always naughty.'

Helen merely smiled at that, her eyes affectionate as they rested on Fiona's lovely face. Later Leon said to her,

'You care a great deal for them, don't you, Helen?'

'I love them,' she returned. 'I'm so glad I stayed, Leon.'

'For only that reason?' He seemed to be tensed as he waited for her reply; she smiled tenderly at him and said softly,

'No, Leon, for another – even more important reason – I'm glad I stayed.'

On the Thursday Helen visited the hairdresser in the village.

'Shampoo and set?' Eleni asked, smiling. 'Or do you want a little off?'

'No, I don't think I'll have it cut, Eleni – just wash it and set it, please.'

'You paint, don't you?' Eleni said later when, the shampooing done, she began to comb out Helen's hair.

'I try to.' Helen gazed at her reflection and wondered whether to try a new hair style. Perhaps Leon would not approve, though. He liked her hair as it was.

'You're very good, I've heard.' Helen made no comment and Eleni went on, 'A friend of my aunt has one of your paintings – but of course you must know. It's beautiful, so my aunt says.'

'One of my paintings?' She stared at Eleni through the mirror. 'They can't have.' She had done only the one painting since coming to the island, and her husband had that. 'There's some mistake.'

'I'm sure there isn't.' Eleni now looked puzzled. 'It's of the old mill – the one here in Lapithos. At least, I think that's what Aunt Thespia said.'

'But – but. . . .' Her heart missed a beat, and her face was slowly losing its colour. How silly of her! Leon had been so encouraging over the picture, and hadn't he refused to take any chances with it by leaving it in the outhouse? Yes, there must be some mistake; Leon would never part with her picture. 'Who is this person who says they have a painting of mine?'

'She lives in Nicosia – Paula Maxwell. She used to go to school with my aunt–' Eleni broke off, and the comb became idle in her hand. 'Are you not feeling well, Mrs. Petrou? Can I get you some water?'

Helen shook her head dumbly. The rest of the colour had drained from her face; her heart felt as if it were surrounded by ice. Leon had given her picture to – to that woman. He must still be seeing her, then. But when? He never went out in the evenings now – hadn't done so for weeks, and that was why she had concluded that the friendship was over, why she had believed her husband had begun to care . . . and why she had allowed herself to care.

'Please carry on, Eleni, I'm quite all right.'

'You're sure, Mrs. Petrou? You look dreadfully pale. Perhaps I can phone your husband? Will he fetch the car for you?'

'I shall be all right. Just — just do my hair, please, Eleni.'

How she managed to sit through the ordeal of having her hair set and dried Helen never knew. Several times she felt like getting up, and it was by sheer force of will that she remained until the drying was finished. And yet she had no desire to go home, no wish to see her husband.

'It's my own fault, entirely my own fault,' she quivered, scarcely able to hold back the tears that threatened. After all the vows she had made never to run the risk of being let down a second time, after swearing she would never fall in love again, she had allowed herself to weaken, allowed herself to succumb to her husband's subtle persuasions, and his charms, confidently believing that he cared, that although he had not loved her when he married her, he had come to love her since. And now she knew there was no love in his relationship with her. It was as she had at one time suspected; all he wanted was for her to be his willing slave. Her coldness had hurt his pride and he had determined to have reciprocation from her, no matter what method he was forced to use. And in that method he had been unscrupulous, utterly heartless and insensible to any hurt he might inflict upon her. Helen felt she hated him ... but she hated herself more for her easy surrender. She recalled the way he had almost begged for her embrace, the way he had of making her feel guilty — just as if it were she who were injuring him. In this way he had won her over — and somehow gained her love. But she did not love him now, she told herself. No, she hated him; she would hate him for the rest of her life.

She walked up the hill, her feet dragging. She did not want to go home, but where could she go? The children ... always the children. They had lost both mother and father; they needed her. 'What can I do?' Tears came and she flicked them away. Leon should not know how much she was hurt.

'Darling, is anything wrong?' He was in the drive when she arrived home, polishing the car in readiness for their journey in the morning. 'Helen, my love, what is it?'

The hypocrisy of him! It was unbelievable. Her heart was like a stone enclosed in ice. Would she ever feel again? Her instinct was to hurl at him all she knew, her one desire to tell him he would never again feel her arms about him. But to have one great rift now, with the holiday only hours away. . . . The holiday would naturally be off – and what of the children? No, she could not disappoint them.

'There's nothing wrong with me, Leon.' Without another word she went into the house and he followed her.

'Sweetheart, there is something wrong. Are you ill?'

How could she act convincingly? And yet she must, just until the holiday was over.

'I've a headache,' she owned. And that was true, for the dryer always gave her a headache. 'I shall be all right in a little while. Don't worry about me, Leon.'

'You must lie down.' His firm authoritative manner grated on her nerves. If only she could treat him as he deserved to be treated! 'Come, dear, I'll help you.' He lifted her on to the bed and took off her shoes. Then he pulled a cover over her and closed the shutters, leaving her in the dark. 'Try to sleep, darling. If you can't, give me a call and I'll get you some aspirin.'

Once alone, Helen could no longer control her tears. How could Leon have done this to her? The way he had praised her work, had insisted on having it in the exhibition. The way he had said he wanted it in his office. And how sincere he had made it all sound! That was the result of wide experience, and of course, part of the manoeuvre for bringing about her capitulation. How he must be gloating, congratulating himself on his guile. Well, let him make the most of it, let him enjoy his victory while he may, for an awakening was close at hand.

And then he could go to Paula Maxwell, for she, Helen, would never have him near her again.

To her surprise Helen felt herself drifting into sleep, and dusk had fallen when she awoke. Leon was sitting by the bed and she asked him to open the shutters.

'It's almost dark, dear. You've slept a long while.' How well he contrived to infuse concern into his voice ... and only a few hours ago she would have been deceived by it. He snapped on the light. 'Are you feeling better?'

'Yes, thank you, Leon.' She sat up, helped by his arm at her back. 'Have the children had their meal?'

'Araté gave it to them. Helen dear, we're not going if you don't feel well.'

'Oh, I am well. It was only the headache.'

'You're quite sure?'

She nodded.

'Quite sure. I'm getting up now.'

'You've no need to worry about the children. Araté will see to them.'

'She doesn't like bathing them. No, I must get up.'

But there was no doubt the shock had done something to her, for she remained pale, and she found at dinner that she could scarcely eat a thing. Leon's concern was as pronounced as he could make it, and a terrible bitterness filled her at the idea that, had this been genuine, she could have crept into his arms and found comfort on his breast. But had he been genuine she would never have received this shock in the first place.

The following morning the children were running about at six o'clock; Leon was far from pleased, telling them to go back to bed, and be quiet.

'Do you feel up to it?' he asked, realizing Helen was awake. 'If you don't feel better than you did yesterday then we're not going.' He held her close, and with that familiar gentleness. How could he be such a hypocrite? Could there possibly be some explanation? Even if Leon were in love with Paula why should he give her the painting? And why should she want it? It suddenly did not make sense. No woman would want a picture that her lover's wife had painted. And yet how had Paula come by the painting unless it had been given to her by Leon? Helen felt his hand caressingly stroke her cheek. So tender, so gentle. . . . Should she ask him about the picture? Could the mystery be cleared up by some quite simple explanation? Supposing, though, that he were guilty? Then there must be a rift – one big row, in fact, and that was what Helen strove to avoid, for the sake of the children. Their voices were heard again, despite the stern warning from their uncle. Excited voices, impatient voices. . . .

They spent the first day with Leon's mother, leaving after tea and booking in at a hotel, at Ktima, the modern capital of Paphos District. The children were allowed to stay up quite late, but once they were in bed Leon suggested a walk. It was a lovely night, a typical eastern night, with a clear purple sky and a crescent moon floating over the sea. Behind them rose the foothills of the Troodos mountains, and higher up, the steep-sided ridges, blurred and indistinct in the soft purple light from a star-filled sky. The sea was calm and the only sound was that of the waves gently lapping the shore. They walked in silence, and Helen wondered if Leon sensed the change in her. For, despite her endeavours, she could not act as if nothing had happened, could not look or speak to him in that tender way which had come naturally to her of late. If he did sense the change he made no comment on it; perhaps he thought she was still off colour, though when he asked her during the afternoon she had stated quite emphatically that she felt quite well.

'The sea's so smooth.' Leon broke the silence at last, stopping to gaze out over the water. 'We'll spend the morning on the sands, and do some swimming. Then in the afternoon we can take the car and drive into the Paphos forest.'

'Is it a long drive? Will the children enjoy it?'

'You will enjoy it.' He took her hand and gave it a little squeeze. 'This isn't just for the children, you know. They'll enjoy themselves on the sands in the morning, and if the afternoon's not so much to their liking then it can't be helped.'

Helen looked up, trying to read his expression, but it was not possible in the dark. How could he put on an act like this? She began to tell herself it was quite impossible when suddenly all that Gregory had done flashed back to her. For a whole year he had deceived her, and so cleverly had he carried out that deception that not the faintest hint of suspicion had entered into her. His attitude towards her had remained the same as always; there had been no sharp words, no unkindness, no quarrels. And her own case was by no means unique. That sort of thing was happening all the time. No, she was not mistaken – it was just that Leon was so adept in the art of deception that it was difficult to believe he was deceiving her at all.

For the children the holiday was a great adventure. They enjoyed every moment of it, and although for Helen it was an ordeal and a strain, she was glad she had come. The children needed the change, for they hadn't had a holiday for some years, and had she disappointed them she would never have forgiven herself. But her own misery was sometimes almost more than she could bear, for she herself had been looking forward as eagerly as a child to this holiday. They would go away as a family, that was what Leon had said, and Helen had visualized such happiness, such bliss in her new relationship with her husband.

And she had not enjoyed a moment of it.

They spent the last morning on the sands, in a lovely little bay to the west of Paphos. Chippy could swim, and Leon had been teaching Fiona at every opportunity. They had all become even more tanned and were glowing with health.

'I wish we weren't going home – must we, Uncle Leon?' Fiona leant against him and looked up pleadingly. 'Can't we stay another day?'

'I'm afraid not, Fiona. But we shall come again – perhaps in a few weeks' time.' He turned to Helen. 'How about it? Would you care to?'

'Yes. . . .' She lowered her head to hide the frown that had appeared at his words. She could never endure another ordeal such as this. Besides, on their return she was going to tell Leon what she knew. There would be no more holidays after that.

'You don't sound too sure, Helen. Haven't you enjoyed yourself?' No endearments during the last couple of days, she had noticed, and the reappearance of that harshness about his mouth and eyes had warned her that he had an inkling something was wrong.

'Yes, I've enjoyed it,' she lied, aware of the anxiety in Fiona's eyes. 'I think we've all had a wonderful time. Am I right, Chippy?'

Her words were forced, and stiff. Naturally this did not register with the children, but Leon's eyes sharpened.

'Yes, we've had a wonderful time. And I don't mind going home if we can come again soon. You promise, Uncle Leon?'

'I promise, Chippy,' he returned, and looked steadily at his wife. He was telling her quite plainly that they would take another holiday soon, whether she liked it or not, and in spite of herself her heartbeats quickened. She had taken it for granted that things would go her way from now on, that, with her knowledge of her husband's duplicity, she could dictate the terms. But would it work out that way? Leon had given her no choice before, and there was no reason why he should give her any now. In fact, the more she thought about it the more she realized that the position regarding her marriage was in no way altered. Were they, then, to return to that state existing before she had learned to care for Leon? She looked at him, sitting there on the sand watching her, his mouth set, his eyes hard with that metallic gleam that had set her trembling on more than one occasion.

Had she really for one moment cherished the hope that she could dictate to this dark and austere foreigner who who was her husband? She could almost have laughed at the idea. No, with a sinking heart she accepted the truth, resigned herself to a resumption of Leon's mastery. Nothing was changed by her discovery; life would go on exactly as before.

# CHAPTER EIGHT

ALTHOUGH she had firmly resolved to inform Leon of her discovery over the painting, Helen found herself continually putting it off. The reason, she admitted, was cowardice, for she feared a scene with her husband. He had given her an example of his anger, and of the cruelty resulting from it, and she actually trembled at the prospect of a repetition. It was not as if he would be ashamed, for it was obvious he knew no shame. Also, had not Robert asserted that a Cypriot never excused his conduct? No, she would receive neither apology nor excuse.

And so she dismissed the idea of telling him that she knew where her painting was, for there seemed no sense at all in creating a situation in which she would be the only one to suffer. But naturally her reticence created another kind of situation, for Leon could find no reason for the complete change in her attitude towards him. For a little while he tolerated it, and she had the odd impression that it was pride which prevented him from asking her for a reason for the change. In the end, however, he did broach the subject and at first his manner was controlled, though unmistakably harsh. They had finished their lunch. The children, who were now on the long summer holiday, were staying for a few days with Vasilios and Asmena. So Helen was alone in the sitting-room when Leon came to her. She was reading and, without warning, he took the book from her and flung it on the table.

'I want an explanation, Helen. I think I'm entitled to one, don't you?'

'Explanation?' Why did she have to tremble? He could not harm her. 'I don't know what you mean, Leon.'

'No?' He stood over her, his eyes darkening with a slowly rising anger. But his manner remained controlled. 'Can you deny that a change has come over you? Can you deny that you no longer – want me?'

'Want?' Her chin lifted. 'I've never wanted you—'

'Don't lie! For a short while we were happy. What happened, that's what I want to know? – what I demand to know! Changes like this don't occur without good reason. Tell me the reason and we can discuss it, resolve any differences between us.'

His words merely had the effect of bringing a bitter curve to her lips, and of increasing the contempt she had come to feel for him. Resolve their differences? The coolness of him, demanding an explanation when he was quite outrageously having an affair with his former girlfriend. She would tell him, and risk the consequences Her thoughts were suddenly checked. She had let him see her love ... and he had secretly gloated over his victory. By forcing her to love him he had achieved his desire, that of ensuring her reciprocation. He had desired her love for no other reason. If she told him the truth now he would naturally believe she still loved him, and would conclude that the change in her was the result of hurt and disillusionment. That was not the impression with which she wanted to leave him, far from it. No, why should she tell him? While he was kept guessing his ego would continue to suffer.

'I still don't understand you,' she began lightly. 'Our marriage was contracted without love on either side. We get along tolerably well, Leon, I can't see you have any complaint.'

His eyes became like sharpened steel.

'You haven't answered my question. What has brought about this sudden change in you?'

'What change?' she asked. So cool and calm her voice, but ... oh, how her heart throbbed!

'Don't you play with me! Answer me, or I'll shake you till you do!' He was standing so close, and his fists clenched and unclenched, as if he were itching to carry out his threat. 'You loved me, for a little while—'

'Loved you?' Despite her fear she could not allow those words to pass without interruption. He must be made to believe she had never loved him, but how? She played for time as she said, 'How have you reached a conclusion like that? I've just said there was love on neither side—'

'When we married, yes, I agree. But you did learn to love me. I'm not a fool, Helen, I know you loved me. If you hadn't you could never have – have. . . .' He seemed unable to voice his thoughts, and Helen supplied, with a calmness that amazed her,

'Responded to your love-making?' She was overwhelmed with the desire to hit back, to make him suffer, not only for what he himself had done to her, but also for what Gregory had done to her. And those calmly uttered words gave her the idea. 'But that? – surely you don't attach any importance to it, Leon. There needn't be love, but it's far more pleasant to have it that way, don't you agree?' The angry colour, slowly appearing in his dark countenance, the swift compression of his mouth and the steely glint in his eyes, these should have warned her, but for a brief moment she was blind to danger, blind to everything except the desire to hurt him, or rather, to hurt his pride, for she was convinced that with a man as heartless as this, his pride was the only thing that could be hurt. 'As regards this change you say you've noticed – well, one can't always be consistent when it's an act. Besides, one tends to become bored. . . .' Helen tailed off and for a while there was no sound, except for the incessant chirping of the cicadas drifting in through the open door of the verandah. But the silence was so frightening that she rose unsteadily to her feet and attempted to reach the door. Leon's grip enclosed her wrist, bringing her back with a jerk that sent a pain right through her shoulder.

'So that was all it was? A convincing act – is that what you're telling me?'

'Leon, you're hurting me—'

'Answer my question, or I'll—' But he seemed unable to control himself another moment and he shook her unmercifully. 'An act, you say! Well, mark my words, you'll live to regret it. No woman makes that sort of fool of me and gets away with it!' He towered above her, his merciless grip still on her arms. All colour had left Helen's face and her whole body trembled from his rough handling of her. He wasn't human, she thought, recalling that she had once before reached this conclusion. But through the cloud of fear that enveloped her brain emerged the sure knowledge that she had achieved her object. He honestly believed himself to have been deceived, believed she had merely been acting a part – had even been bored at times with his lovemaking. What a blow to his pride that must be! Let him shake her, let him vent his entire fury on her – it was worth it to have this revenge on him. Nevertheless, she still trembled and she did wonder what he meant by saying she would live to regret it.

She looked up and swiftly lowered her head again. His lips were drawn back in a snarl and for one terrifying moment she expected to be subjected to his primitive cruelty again, but to her astonishment and relief he suddenly flung her from him and strode from the room. A few moments later she heard the car door slam, then the noise of the engine fading as the car proceeded down the hill.

Where had he gone? No need to ask that. Helen sat down on the chair and put her face in her hands. She still trembled and her heart was beating so loudly that she could actually hear it. The house was so quiet. . . . Araté and Nikos never worked on Sunday afternoons, and suddenly Helen felt an urge to leave the house, felt she could not bear to be alone in it. Where could she go? If only she had known she would have kept the children at home. For the first time she was conscious of being a long way from her friends, from those few people who would gladly have opened their doors to her, sincere in their welcome. Here she had no one, no one except her husband's relations, and Trudy. But she could not bring herself to go to the flat, for Trudy must instantly guess that something was wrong. And yet there was nowhere else. . . .

Robert was some time answering the phone and, on learning she had brought him down from the little studio he had built for himself on the roof, Helen hastily apologized.

'That's all right,' he returned breezily. 'I was intending ringing you later. That Englishman – Mr. Crawley – has sent me a key to the house and asked me to contact you. He wants us to get started right away as he's hoping to move in by the autumn.' A slight pause and then, 'I don't suppose you're free now? I could come over if you are; this work I'm doing isn't that important. Just some things for the art shop in Kyrenia.'

'I am free, yes, Robert, and I'd like to see you and discuss the work for Mr. Crawley. You can come at once, you say?'

'Yes . . . but your husband? I have an idea I'm not too popular with him?' Helen could almost see the grimace on Robert's large, good-natured face.

'Leon is out,' she submitted quietly. 'I don't expect him back until late tonight.'

A little silence followed her words, and then Robert said casually,

'I'll be over in about half an hour, then. And I'll bring the key with me and we can drive out and see what we have to do.' A slight hesitation before he added, 'Perhaps we could go somewhere for tea?'

146

'That would be nice -- yes, Robert, I'd like to do that.'

True to his word, Robert arrived exactly half an hour later. Helen went out to fetch some refreshment and she was in the kitchen when she heard the telephone ringing. She went to answer it and was surprised to see Robert with the receiver in his hand. She was more surprised when, instead of handing it to her as she expected, he kept it against his ear. The voice at the other end was loud and shrill. Helen heard every word quite clearly.

'—and Leon, we'll go in your car, it's much more comfortable than mine. Bring some sandwiches too, and a flask, for we'll be out in the wilds at times and you know how difficult it is to get anything.' The voice stopped speaking. Eyeing Helen with a most odd expression on his face, Robert covered the receiver and hissed,

'An old flame of your husband's – Paula Maxwell. Thinks she's speaking to Leon. What must I do?'

Pale, but composed, Helen took the receiver from him and said politely,

'Mrs. Petrou speaking. I'm afraid my husband isn't in. Can I take a message?' She waited, looking at Robert and wondering if she had been cut off. But Paula spoke at last and her voice was much quieter than before.

'Leon isn't in, you say? Have you any idea when he'll back?'

'I'm sorry, no.' Helen glanced at the clock; her heart gave a little jerk as she realized that her husband had had ample time to reach Nicosia – were that his destination. 'I can't say when he'll be back. Can I take a message?' she asked again.

'No, thank you. I'll get in touch with him— Oh, he's here now.' A pause and then, 'Who is the man, Mrs. Petrou?' The voice was low and silky; Helen experienced both fear and indignation. She dismissed her fear and said shortly,

'That's my business, Miss Maxwell.'

'I'll bet it is,' came the rather staggering retort. 'But don't have any fear, I'll not say a word to Leon.'

Replacing the receiver with a hand that trembled visibly, Helen turned to Robert. Before she could speak he apologized for answering the phone.

'I was just going out to the car to fetch my cigarettes; it started to ring and I picked up the receiver automatically. I tried to tell her I wasn't Leon, but she went on about something — I really couldn't tell you what because I was so staggered. You see,' he added, an odd note creeping into his voice, 'as soon as she said her name I remembered this Paula Maxwell who'd been going around with him quite a lot before he married you.'

'Does everybody know about her?' The words came with difficulty, for her throat felt dry, but she had to say them, even though she knew very well what Robert's answer would be.

'They were extremely good friends,' he submitted reluctantly. 'Yes, Helen, I'm afraid everyone does know about her.' Helen returned to the kitchen and he followed her. 'It's not my business, I know, but what in the name of heaven is happening? If he wanted her then why the devil did he marry you?'

She managed at last to swallow the dryness in her throat as she told him, quite candidly, why she and Leon had married. A whistle of astonishment left his lips and he stared at her in disbelief.

'No ... it couldn't happen like that!' Trudy, she reflected, had said something of the sort, too.

'Shall we have our drinks?' she said, taking up the tray. 'We'll sit on the verandah, it's far more pleasant than being indoors.'

'You're very calm,' he observed, taking the glass she handed to him. He pulled out a chair for her and she sat down. 'No love on either side, I take it?'

'That's right, no love on either side.' She watched him sit down and lift the glass to his lips. He was good-looking, she thought mechanically. How odd that he appeared so satisfied with his bachelor existence. She looked out to the sea. So calm, not even a ripple. Instinctively she turned her gaze to the mountains; rough and rocky tracks ran through them. You followed these little roads and you found yourself out in the wilds. . . . Where were they now? On their way to some familiar haunt up there in the mountains? Perhaps it was not the mountains, for there were out-of-the-way places all over the island – romantic places like little dells or lonely beaches. . . . It became too much of an effort to hold back the tears and, draining her glass, she put it on the tray and got up from her chair.

'I'll go and tidy my hair and fetch my bag.'

'What time will the kiddies be back?' he asked, picking up the tray and carrying it to the kitchen.

'They're not coming back,' she called from the bedroom. 'Leon's aunt and uncle are having them for a few days.'

'Oh, then how about making a nice long afternoon and evening of it? We could have a look at the house, and see what's to be done, then go for a swim, and end up having dinner somewhere.' He was standing outside the bedroom door, waiting for her to come out. She had put on the dress Leon had bought her and another whistle left Robert's lips as he surveyed her admiringly from head to foot. He took the beach bag from her hand and continued to stare at her.

'Some men are fools,' was his only comment as, moving to let her pass, he then followed her out to the hall.

'I don't know where the key is— Oh, it's here.' Robert took it from her and, locking the door behind them, he handed Helen the key.

The house was a beautiful white villa standing on the

hillside above Kyrenia. Money had obviously not been considered when planning it, and on entering the panelled hall Helen could not help giving a little gasp of admiration.

'It's going to be beautiful when it's finished,' she breathed, even forgetting her unhappiness for the moment as she gazed round in appreciation. 'Where will our paintings be?'

Robert had all the instructions and they walked round, finding the panels in which the paintings were to appear.

'It's going to be fun doing this sort of work,' Robert said with enthusiasm. 'And we can do it together. I'll pick you up in the car and drop you off when we return.'

What, she wondered, would Leon have to say to an arrangement like that? He would not approve, that was a certainty, but as his approval or disapproval no longer interested her she gave the matter no further thought.

'Murals are really going to look splendid here. I'm terribly eager to get started. When can you begin, Helen?'

'Any time – though I don't know how I'll go on while the children are at home. When they return to school, though, I can come every morning – except at the weekends, of course.'

'But the children are away at present? How long for?'

'A few days – that was the original intention, but Asmena is so fond of them, and she and Vasilios have none of their own so I fully expect they'll ask Leon if they can have Chippy and Fiona for a little while longer.'

'Then we might make a start right away?'

'Yes, I don't see why not.'

It was settled that Robert should pick her up at nine o'clock the following morning and they would go into town for all the necessary materials. Then they could begin work right away.

'There's a lovely little café on the hillside nearby where we can have our meals. This is going to be fun, Helen.'

Fun? Would anything ever be fun again? True, she was looking forward to making a start on the paintings, but she lacked her initial enthusiasm, for her work would now be merely a diversion, something to help her forget the misery in her heart.

She and Robert went to a secluded part of the beach six miles from Kyrenia, and spent a couple of hours in the sea, or sunbathing on the lovely golden sands. Yet the whole time her thoughts were with Leon and Paula. Where were they, and what were they doing? She supposed they would stay out late – or go back to Paula's home.

'Shall we go in the water again?' she said swiftly, for was sure she was going to cry.

'By all means.' He took her hand and they walked towards the sea. The action brought back the memory of another occasion, that time on Famagusta sands when Leon had taken her hand in just this same way, holding it tenderly, and they had walked to the water's edge. She had not known at the time that she was so near to caring, and yet she had enjoyed the companionship, she recalled, and the beginning of a great happiness had welled up within her. And how fleeting that happiness. It was gone; she had been awakened from her dream.

'I don't know how you feel,' said Robert half an hour later, 'but I think I've had enough. How about some tea, a nice run around the countryside, and then dinner?'

'Yes, I'd like that.'

They took it in turns to change in the car. Helen wrapped her wet costume in the towel and put it in her bag. Then she combed her hair and Robert held the mirror while she put a little colour on her face.

'Shall we go to the harbour for tea?' Robert handed back her mirror and she put it in her bag. 'Or would you like somewhere more secluded?'

'Somewhere more secluded,' she returned without hesitation. There were far too many people on the harbour on Sunday afternoons. She was almost sure to be seen by someone from Lapithos, and although she no longer cared about her husband's opinion of her, she had no desire to have her name bandied about by the villagers.

After tea they drove into the hills; darkness fell and Robert suggested a well-known restaurant for dinner. Helen hesitated and immediately Robert said,

'Wherever we go we could be seen, Helen. How would you like to come back to my place, and we'll knock up a meal of our own?'

Again she hesitated. She really ought to go home, but if she did it would only be to spend the evening alone.

'That's a good idea, Robert. Yes, I'd like to do that. And I'm very interested to see what you've done with your little house.'

'It's so tiny,' he owned, 'but I like it. I hadn't much money and in fact I'm still doing small renovations. However, it's fairly comfortable, and I do have a fridge.'

'I think you've made a wonderful job of it!' she exclaimed, on entering the house. She was in the kitchen, but through a high white archway was a little dining-recess. 'I love this archway – and the ceiling. I haven't seen one of these Turkish rush ceilings before, although I've heard of them.'

'They're not rushes, they're bamboos – interwoven. And the supports are merely tree-trunks that have been stripped of the bark. And the archway, that was already here; I just had to have it reinforced and then I painted it white. I like the white, don't you? This is the bathroom, and this is a little utility room.' Helen followed him, wondering where the sitting-room could be, for there were no more doors. 'And now for upstairs.' He led the way up the narrow spiral staircase. There was one room only. It was furnished as a bed-sitting-room.

'Is this all?' She blinked at him and he laughed at her expression.

'Originally it had one up and one down. I've made the three tiny rooms downstairs, and kept this as a large bed-sitting-room. There really wasn't any other way to work it out.'

'It's a wonderful idea,' she agreed, walking into the room and glancing up at the ceiling. It was the same as that downstairs and looked extremely attractive.

'I feel almost as if I've preserved an ancient monument,' he laughed. 'This house is hundreds of years old.'

'Well, you've made it very comfortable.' She met his gaze, wondering again at his being so satisfied to live alone. He had spent a good deal of time and money on this house – and it would never do for more than one person. There was no possibility of building on, either, for it was in the middle of a row.

'Come and see my studio,' he invited. 'You have to go out through this window, and climb a sort of ladder – but it's quite safe.'

The view was breathtaking.

'No wonder you can paint up here,' she gasped, looking from the low wide windows to the surrounding mountains and sea. 'And it's so quiet!'

'That's what I like. I must be quiet at times – not only when I'm painting. Some people need to be alone, and I'm one of those people. That's why I don't bother about marriage; it would be selfish of me to expect any girl to put up with my odd ways.'

How sensible, and how considerate. Few men would be as considerate as he, she thought, recalling with bitterness the selfishness of the two men she had known.

They came downstairs and Robert showed her the fridge.

'Pick out what you want,' he said accommodatingly, 'while I see to the table.'

'Shall we have something cooked?' There were several kinds of meat in the fridge, but also plenty of salads, and those outsize tomatoes that were far more delicious than any others Helen had ever tasted.

'No, don't cook in that lovely dress,' he advised. 'Let's make do with cold meats and salad.' And of course there was plenty of fruit.

To her surprise Helen enjoyed the meal. Robert was good company while at the same time giving the impression that he was, basically, a deep thinker. What Helen liked about him was that, after his first surprised inquiry, he had not again mentioned Leon, or the peculiar circumstances of her marriage to him. In fact, he treated her as a friend, liking her for her own sake, and allowing her to keep her private life as something apart. They would get on well together in the work they were soon to share, she concluded, and to her surprise found herself eagerly looking forward to having his company.

Although her action in coming out with Robert was one of defiance, Helen had no desire to endure another scene with Leon so soon after that of the early afternoon and at nine o'clock she asked Robert to take her home.

He left her at the gate and to her relief she saw that the bungalow was in complete darkness. She let herself in with the key and went straight to bed.

The following morning Leon went off early to join the convoy and after helping Araté with the chores Helen got herself ready and was waiting when Robert called at nine o'clock.

'Shall we have to take the longer route?' she asked, sitting beside him in the car.

'I think so. I'm allowed through, being English, but I don't know how you're fixed, being married to a Greek.'

And so he took the longer route and it was after ten when at last the capital was reached.

Their shopping took rather longer than they expected and Robert suggested they stay in Nicosia for lunch.

'That will be a nice change,' she agreed, and they went to the Hilton.

The first person Helen saw was Paula Maxwell; she was sitting over in a corner, at a table for two. Helen's heart seemed to turn right over. She recalled that other occasion when she had seen her husband with Paula here at lunch time, but she had not for one moment expected such a coincidence as this to occur.

'Robert,' she faltered, aware that Paula had seen her and was staring with interest at her companion, 'do you mind if we go s-somewhere else? Paula is here – w-with my husband.'

'Paula and Leon?' He frowned and looked about him. 'Here?'

'Over in the corner.' Helen knew the colour had left her face. Where was her husband? He would be here in a moment or two, of that she was sure.

'Please, Robert, I don't want to see Leon.'

'How do you know she's with Leon? I don't see any sign of him. Oh, to the devil; here, take a chair!'

'No, Robert—'

'If he can lunch with her then you can lunch with me.' Robert almost pushed her into the chair, and she made no further protest, for although she was some distance from Paula, she could see the smile on her face and sense the other girl's amusement at her discomfiture.

'Oh, how silly of me!' Helen had been watching the table, waiting with wildly beating heart for Leon to appear. But the man lunching with Paula was elderly. He sat down opposite to her and drew some papers from his pocket. Paula leant over and together they perused them. 'It's not Leon, after all.'

'No?' Robert turned his head. 'There you are, all that panic for nothing. That's a potential customer, I expect.'

'What does she sell?'

'She's an estate agent. Didn't you know?'

Of course – Phil had mentioned it.

'Yes, I did – I remember now.' Her eyes were on Paula again. She was certainly attractive, but there was a certain poise about her that gave her a hint of arrogance. Well suited to a man like Leon ... and an estate agent. They would have much in common.

'She probably brings all her clients here,' Robert said, handing Helen the menu. 'Atmosphere, you know. It's the thing to soften up your customers with a slap-up lunch or dinner. I expect your husband does the same – brings his customers here, I mean – sure to, in fact.'

Yes, her husband did come to the Hilton, but not always with customers.

On the way back they made their intended detour and went to the house, leaving their paints there and a small spirit stove which Robert had bought, saying they must have their coffee breaks to keep them going. They stayed a long while, measuring up and doing the preliminary work in preparation for their start the following morning.

Leon was in when Helen arrived home; he glanced up from his newspaper and asked her where she had been.

'Into Nicosia, to buy my paints – for the house.'

'You've just arrived back? Why didn't you come to the office and ride home with me?'

So coolly he could ask why she had not come to the office, when he must know full well that she would wonder what had happened to her painting. What excuse would he give, were she to ask him about it? No doubt he would have some plausible explanation ready, though what it could be she could not possibly think.

'Robert took me into town. He had to buy his paints, too. We've left them at the house.' She stood by the couch, looking down at him, recalling that this was their first conversation since he had strode away and left her after their quarrel yesterday.

His mouth had compressed and Helen steeled herself for what was to come. Would life always be like this? Would Leon always be able to set her heart racing with fear every time she did something of which he might not approve?

'What time did you go into town?'

'Robert came for me at nine o'clock.' She moved away, finding a chair at the other side of the room, as far from him as possible.

'Nine o'clock. . . .' His eyes flickered almost imperceptibly to his wrist watch. Helen swallowed, her own glance moving to the clock on the wall. 'You've been together the whole of the day?'

Helen cleared her throat.

'Well, not – not—'

'It's now half-past five,' he informed her softly.

'We had to go to the house, to leave the paints.'

'You've just told me that.' Slowly and deliberately he folded his newspaper and laid it on the small table at his elbow. Both his words and his actions had a disconcerting effect on her and her hands began to twitch nervously in her lap.

'We had some preliminary work to do,' she explained. 'We're making a start in the morning.' He might just as well know all, she decided. It would save another scene like this tomorrow. 'I expect to be out all day.'

'With this Englishman?'

'With Robert, yes, Leon.' She paused, noticing the tiny white lines slowly creeping up under the dark tan of his face. 'We both have work to do at the house, so naturally we shall be there together.'

'And you expect to be out all day, do you?'

She nodded.

'Yes, that's right.'

Leon stood up and came across the room towards her.

'I've changed my mind about allowing you to do this work,' he said calmly. 'You can write to Mr. Crawley and tell him you are not now at liberty to assist him.'

'Write—?' Her eyes widened incredulously. 'You expect me to do that? – to let him down, after having promised?' She shook her head. 'I can't, Leon. I discussed it with you at the beginning, when he asked me to do the work, and you made no objection then.'

'The circumstances were different.'

'In what way different?' she wanted to know, and a steely glint entered his eyes.

'I don't think I need answer that question,' he said curtly, and, after a pause, 'I mean what I say. You're not to do this work. Understand?'

She sat straight up in her chair.

'No, Leon, I don't understand.' Her voice was low and steady. She met his gaze unflinchingly. 'I refuse to take orders like that from you. I've a right to a certain amount of freedom. I'll please myself over this; the promise was made to Mr. Crawley and it will be kept.' Her husband's dark eyes began to smoulder, but for once Helen was determined not to be browbeaten. In any case, the work was important to her; it would help her forget, for a time at least, the pain and disillusionment for which he himself was responsible. Even at the risk of another violent scene she added, on a distinct note of defiance, 'Robert is calling for me in the morning – he'll be doing so every morning while the children are away – and I shall go with him. I'm sorry if you dislike the idea of my working with him, but—' she spread her hands – 'there's nothing you can do about it.'

The silence of amazement descended on the room, it seemed for a moment as if her defiance would prove too much for Leon's self-control. In his eyes lay a threat; his hands moved as if itching to strike her, and despite her bravado Helen experienced a renewed fluttering of her nerves. And then his anger died, to be replaced by an inflexibility that was even more pronounced. His relentless attitude, and the uncompromising line of his mouth, convinced her of the futility of her efforts at defiance. He meant to have his way and she wondered what plan he was conjuring up in order to enforce her obedience to his will. But how could he enforce her obedience to his will? She was allowing her fear of him to overcome her common sense. Short of locking her up there were no means whatsoever by which he could prevent her from going out with Robert in the morning.

'Is that your last word?' he inquired softly at last.

Helen nodded unhappily. How different it all was from what she expected when Mr. Crawley had requested her to do the work for him. She had been so happy, and Leon had appeared to be so proud of her. Even his flash of ill-humour at the idea of Robert's working with her had increased her happiness – for she had taken it for jealousy.

A curious little lump rising in her throat made speech difficult, but at length she managed to say,

'I must do the work, Leon. Not only have I promised, but it will also give me pleasure.'

'Pleasure, eh?' His teeth were together; his manner became even more inflexible as he stared down at her for a while, his dark eyes thoughtful. 'You'll enjoy spending the whole day in that house with your friend from England – that's what you're telling me, I take it?'

'You know that isn't what I meant. I enjoy painting and – and I've been looking forward to doing this work.' She looked up at him, but he was completely unmoved by the hint of tears in her eyes.

'I believe I warned you, on a previous occasion, that I am not willing to have my wife's name linked with that of this Robert. I meant it then and I mean it now. Either you defer to my request willingly, or I take measures to ensure that you do so. The choice is entirely yours.'

She flushed angrily and her chin went up.

'I won't meekly accept your orders!' she flashed. 'And as for taking measures to ensure my turning down that work – well, the idea's ridiculous! You can't very well lock me in the house.'

'No, my dear,' he agreed softly. 'That is hardly what I have in mind.' Without another word he left the room, and as on an earlier occasion she heard the car move out of the drive.

She was in the kitchen, helping Araté with the dinner when she again heard the car in the drive. Almost immediately the children burst into the room.

'Aunt Helen!' Fiona bounded across the floor and hugged her tightly. 'We liked Aunt Asmena – but we were so glad when Uncle Leon came for us!'

'I'm never going away again – not without you,' stated Chippy emphatically. 'Don't make us, will you, Uncle Leon?' Chippy turned to his uncle and Leon smiled down at him.

'No, Chippy, I'll never make you go away,' and then, quizzically, 'I thought you were enjoying yourselves.'

'Oh, we have enjoyed ourselves,' interposed Fiona swiftly, as if realizing they were not being very appreciative of Asmena's hospitality. 'But we love you two best of all, and so we wanted to come home.'

# CHAPTER NINE

THE days dragged, for the children were out playing most of the time, and Helen's indignation against her husband gradually increased until it reached gigantic proportions. What right had he to domineer over her like this? She was English, not one of these servile eastern women whose lot it was to have no interests other than the care of her husband and children. Much as she loved Chippy and Fiona, she still felt entitled to a little leisure time in which to enjoy her hobby. Besides, why should Leon be out all the while, leaving her with them? For, since their quarrel, he had never once stayed home in the evening. On Sundays, too, he was out – out with Paula Maxwell, she had no doubt of that. When Helen complained about being left so much, Leon coldly reminded her that she was here, primarily, to look after the children.

With the deliberate intention of forcing him to remain at home, at least for one evening, Helen invited Trudy and Tasos to dinner. They had already paid one visit to the bungalow, and Helen and Leon and the children had been invited to the flat in return. Tasos and Leon had got along fine, and with this in mind Helen did not expect for one moment that her husband would refuse to stay in.

'Tomorrow evening?' His tone was cool, his gaze indifferent. 'I have an appointment. I shall be out until about ten.'

'An appointment?' she queried, her blue eyes flashing. 'In the evening?'

'In the evening.' He was standing with his hands in his pockets, his face marred by the harshness that had recently become a permanent part of him. 'There are people who are not free during the day and therefore have to see me in the evenings.'

Such as Paula, whose business kept her occupied throughout the day.

'I've invited Trudy and Tasos; surely you can stay in for once?'

'Had you made it any other evening I could have arranged it, but not tomorrow; I'm sorry.'

He was not sorry at all. If he were, he could quite simply tell his lady friend that he had another appointment – or tell her the truth. But he would never do that, Helen concluded, for Paula would be far from pleased at the knowledge that Leon preferred to stay at home. And she was quite sure he lied when he stated that, were it any other evening, he could have arranged it. That was merely an excuse.

'They'll feel terribly slighted,' Helen persevered, despite her conviction that she wasted her time. 'And me – I shall feel most embarrassed. What can I say?'

He moved impatiently.

'Why didn't you consult me before inviting them?'

She could hardly give the answer to that, hardly own that she had deliberately sent the invitation first so that Leon would be forced to remain at home.

'I suppose I should have done so,' she admitted flatly. Although it was against her natural inclination she stared up at him pleadingly. 'It's going to be so difficult for me, Leon.'

A deep sigh left his lips.

'Very well,' he agreed. 'I'll put off my client. But in future please consult me. It is not businesslike to make an appointment and then cancel it at such short notice.'

A hint of bewilderment entered her eyes. He sounded so genuine. Could it be that he wasn't seeing Paula every evening, after all? She shrugged and all her bitterness returned. He was clever; hadn't she already had undeniable proof of it?

162

Trudy and Tasos came early, and the first part of the evening was spent in the garden. The children, excited at the idea of having visitors, refused to go far and their voices and laughter could be heard the whole time.

'Those two are lucky,' Tasos commented, glancing over to where Fiona, on the swing, was being pushed high in the air by Chippy. 'They've lost one father and mother, but found another.' His words brought Helen's glance to that of her husband. There was an ironic twist to his mouth and his eyes were faintly mocking. A complete change had occurred in his attitude towards her since that day, nearly a fortnight ago, when he had so unexpectedly brought the children back from Asmena's. His interest had waned, as had his desire, and there had been a return to the relationship that had existed at the very beginning of their marriage. On first drifting into this way of living, Helen firmly believed it to be what she wanted, for wasn't it what she had expected on first accepting Leon's proposal of marriage? The only thing she resented, she told herself, was his authoritative manner and the peremptory way in which he sometimes spoke to her. Allowed a certain amount of freedom, she believed she could be tolerably content with her lot. But as the days slowly passed Helen became more and more conscious of the restlessness within her, of the gap in her life now that her husband had lost interest in her. And although she squirmed at the admission, there were times when she felt that it were better to have a share of his attention, than not to be noticed at all. If only she had not allowed herself to care, if only she had resisted her husband's subtle persuasions, then this disinterest of his would be more than welcome. But, unfortunately, she had learned to care.

Aware that Trudy's gaze was intently fixed upon her, Helen turned and smiled. Trudy's face cleared. Had she noticed anything? She must not. Helen could not bear it if anyone guessed she no longer held any attraction for her husband.

'Uncle Leon. ...' Fiona's sweet voice drifted over to them. 'Will you come and push me? Chippy won't do it any more.'

'It's my turn, that's why,' he complained as Leon rose from his deck chair and walked over to them. 'She wants it all the time.'

'All right, Fiona, off you come.'

'No. I want you—'

'No?'

'Give me a push first.' She glanced at her uncle from under her long lashes. 'Please,' she added artfully.

'Off!' Fiona obeyed and he gave her a smack.

'O-ooh, that hurt!' Her eyes widened in surprise and she cast him a plaintive look. She rubbed the affected part and ran to her aunt. 'He's cruel – I don't like him any more!'

They all laughed at her expression and she gave them each a baleful glance.

'Poor Fiona!' Helen extended her arms. 'Come and sit on my knee.'

'Baby!' shouted Chippy from the swing. His uncle was pushing him. The breeze caught Leon's hair, tousling it into attractive disorder. Helen watched him over the top of Fiona's head and he turned, sensing her gaze upon him. Swiftly she lowered her eyes, giving her attention to the child.

'He hurt me awful,' she was complaining. 'He's horrid!'

'Nonsense; you're not hurt at all.' Helen sat her more comfortably on her knee.

'I am truly.' Fiona put her arms right round Helen's neck. 'I love you, but I don't love him.'

'I'm sure you love him very much,' put in Trudy, a sort of yearning note creeping into her voice. 'He certainly loves you.'

'He doesn't!' She watched him pushing the swing. 'If he loved me he wouldn't hurt me.'

True, mused Helen. You don't hurt those you love. Not that he had hurt his niece – but it was not Fiona of whom Helen was thinking.

Leaving the swing, Leon came over and stood by Helen's chair, his eyes flickering indifferently over his wife's face and coming to rest on that of his niece.

'What's the matter with you?'

'You've hurt me, and I don't like you now.'

'Sure?' A faintly quizzical note in his voice, but his eyes were serious.

'Yes, I'm sure. I only love Aunt Helen; she never hurts anyone.'

A small silence. For no reason at all Helen felt the colour rise in her cheeks as she met her husband's hard inscrutable gaze.

'Doesn't she, Fiona?' His voice was soft; his eyes never wavered from Helen's flushed countenance.

'No, she doesn't,' asserted Fiona, putting her arms more tightly round Helen's neck. 'She's always kind, and that's why I love her.'

The merest breath of a sigh and then, turning, Leon sat down beside Tasos and the two men became engaged in conversation.

'I'll go and see to dinner,' Helen said a short while later. 'Araté isn't very well and she hasn't been in today.'

'Can I help?' Trudy rose at the same time, but Helen shook her head.

'I have everything ready, and the meal's in the oven. There's just the table—'

'I'll do that,' Trudy offered, following Helen as she went up the steps to the house. 'Are the children having dinner too?'

'No; they'll be going to bed in a little while.'

165

'Won't they be hungry?'

'They've had their tea – and they have milk and biscuits before they go to bed. No, they won't be hungry.'

Trudy saw to the table while Helen busied herself in the kitchen. Then Helen called to Chippy and Fiona. She washed their hands and faces, then they returned to the kitchen, both children protesting that it was much too early to be going to bed.

'It's your usual time,' she reminded them.

'But we've got visitors, and I don't like going to bed when we've got visitors.'

'That's because you're afraid of missing something,' Trudy teased, and again Helen noticed that hint of yearning in her voice. She confided that both she and Tasos wanted children and that if none came along soon they were going to see about adopting one.

'It's surprising how you can come to care for someone else's children,' Helen had said, wondering what she would do if ever Chippy and Fiona were taken from her. They were not legally adopted by their uncle and sometimes their mother would intrude into Helen's thoughts. And always it would be a long while before Helen was able to shake off the hint of fear and dejection which these thoughts inspired.

'Can't we stop up and have dinner with you?' Chippy asked hopefully, eyeing the cold sweets, and the fruit, which Helen had set out in silver dishes ready to be put on the table.

'Certainly not; you never stay up.'

'How old do you have to be before you can stay up?' Fiona's small finger hovered over the cream on the trifle and Helen gave her a stern and warning glance.

'That needn't trouble you for a long time yet. Now, come and get your biscuits and milk.' Helen had set out their supper on a small table by the window and both children sat down.

166

'If we ask Uncle Leon he might let us,' Fiona began, nibbling at her biscuit.

'Might let you what?' Leon appeared from the verandah and went over to the fridge.

'We want to stay up,' she explained. 'I'm not tired and neither is Chippy, so can we have dinner with you?' She glanced at him coaxingly and a half smile touched his mouth.

'You're asking favours – when you don't love me any more?'

'Oh, but I do now,' she quickly declared. 'I love you as much as Aunt Helen.'

'I'm relieved.' He opened the door of the fridge, glanced inside, and frowned. 'Haven't we any canned beer?'

'It's right at the back.' Helen came over to him. 'Shall I get it?'

'I can get it if I know where it is.'

'These will have to be moved.' Helen began moving things out of the way and at last the beer could be seen. They both reached for it together and their hands touched. Leon swiftly withdrew his, leaving her to bring out the cans. She passed them to him; he took them without a word and, after getting the opener and the glasses, he returned to the garden.

Helen stood by the fridge, gently rubbing her hand where Leon's had touched it, and a sudden hurtful prick at the back of her eyes caused her to blink rapidly. Was it only a few weeks since he had caressed her so tenderly? – since he would seize every opportunity of taking her hand or putting a gentle arm around her shoulder? And now he could not bear even the merest touch of her fingers on his.

'I've done the table.' Trudy came back to the kitchen and glanced around. 'Is there anything else I can do?'

'No, thank you, Trudy. Everything's ready. Come,

167

Fiona, stop wasting time. Drink your milk, Chippy.'

'We haven't had a bath,' Chippy reminded Helen. 'Are you coming to give us one?'

'Oh, yes, I forgot that.' Fiona waited expectantly for Helen's reply to her brother's question.

'Not tonight,' she said. 'You've had a wash.'

'Uncle Leon says you must never go to bed without having a bath.'

'And so you shouldn't, normally. But I haven't time tonight. Had Araté been here I should have bathed you. As it is, you won't take any harm for once.'

A deep sigh left Fiona's lips, and Trudy laughed.

'Anything so they can stay up a little while longer, isn't it?'

But at last the children were in bed. The dinner was served and the evening passed pleasantly, with neither of their visitors guessing at the rift that existed between Helen and her husband. To Helen's relief Leon relaxed the familiar austere manner he had recently adopted towards her. At times he would be merely courteous and polite, but at others his manner was affectionate, his smile almost tender.

'You must come to us,' Tasos invited as they were saying good night. He and Trudy were in the car, and Helen and Leon standing beside it. When shall it be? Next week some time?'

'I'm not sure— Look, can we leave it for a day or two, and I'll tell Helen when I'm free?'

'Of course.'

Did this mean he was not going to return the visit? Helen wondered dismally. She hoped Leon would not do anything to spoil her friendship with Trudy in the way he had with Robert. Robert had lost patience with her since she had let herself be dictated to over the work at the villa, and he would not give her the merest nod when they happened to see each other in the village.

'I'd love the kiddies to come some time,' Trudy was saying, her head out of the window. 'I'll tell you what — why not bring them to the flat when you come on Friday?'

'I don't know—' Helen hesitated. 'They can be quite boisterous, Trudy, and you have such lovely things.'

'So have you,' Tasos put in. 'We don't consider our place to be a show house. We like *people* in it, never mind about the *things*.'

'But I'd hate them to break anything of yours,' she began, when Leon interrupted her.

'I can't imagine they'd misbehave, Helen.' He shook his head. 'No, I don't think you need worry. We'll all go down to Nicosia together on Friday.'

'Fine; see you later in the week, then. Good night.'

'Good night, Trudy. Good night, Tasos.' Helen and Leon stood in the drive until the car passed out of sight round a bend lower down the hill, then they went indoors again.

Somehow it seemed to her that the little social event had eased the tension between them, and she said conversationally,

'I did enjoy having them, didn't you, Leon?'

'It was a most pleasant evening,' he agreed, yawning. 'Your meal was excellent.'

'Thank you.' She smiled at him and sat down, almost willing him to do the same. What was the matter with her? This could only lead to her own humiliation. Leon had no further use for her ... surely she had more pride than to beg for his favours. But if only he would be kind! She could not bear to go on like this, not the way she felt. For it was easy to say she no longer cared — but much more difficult to convince herself of the truth of this.

'It's late.' Leon stood by the bookcase, his hands in his pockets, looking across the room at her. 'I think I'll turn in. Good night, Helen.'

Her heart sank. But what did she really want? Helen could not have said.

'Good night, Leon,' she quivered. 'You're right – it is late. I'm – I'm going, too.'

'I should. You look tired.' He walked to the door. 'Good night,' he said again, and went out.

Aunt Chrisoula telephoned the following day. She asked for Leon and when Helen told her he was at the office she said irascibly,

'No, he isn't! He's never there when I ring. What's he doing about my bungalow, that's what I want to know?'

'Your bungalow? Has he managed to find one for you, then?'

'I've told you, that's what I want to know. He said over a week ago that he's seen the very thing, but that the price was too high. I expected he was going to get it reduced for me.'

'And hasn't he been in touch with you since?'

'I've neither seen him nor heard from him,' she replied irritably. 'Where is he, anyway? Why isn't he at his office?'

'I don't know, Aunt Chrisoula. Perhaps he's out on business—'

'What, every day? Just you tell him I want to see him, tonight!'

'He's usually late home, but I'll tell him when he does come in. If it's not too late he'll probably be over. Otherwise it will have to be another time—'

'Another time? When? Look here, Helen, what's going on? Why doesn't he get home early? Where does he go?'

Helen hesitated. It was plain that Aunt Chrisoula was puzzled by her nephew's conduct, and Helen debated on whether or not to try and make excuses for Leon. But what could she say? It would seem that there was only one course open to her: honesty.

'I have no idea where Leon goes,' she admitted. 'He doesn't discuss his business affairs with me.'

'Business – business! Are you telling me he's doing business at night?' Unable to answer that, Helen remained silent and the old lady went on, a distinct note of suspicion in her voice, 'He never was one for frequenting the restaurants and cafés, not regularly, that is, so he must be somewhere else. Now where, that's what I want to know?'

An impatient sigh left Helen's lips.

'I'm afraid I can't help you, Aunt Chrisoula. I'll give Leon the message when he comes in, and I expect he'll be in touch with you as soon as he can.'

'He'd better! I want to see that husband of yours, Helen, so just you make that quite clear to him!'

A trembling hand replaced the receiver. Leon was never at the office, and he was never home until late in the evening. He might just as well go and live with Paula Maxwell! Angry tears started to Helen's eyes, and although she tried to stem them she was soon weeping into her handkerchief. Fiona chose that moment to come in from the garden; she stared at Helen in astonishment and then flung her arms around her waist.

'Why are you crying? Oh, please don't cry. Are you sad, Aunt Helen?'

Helen dried her eyes and with an effort produced a wan little smile.

'No, darling, it's nothing. Run along and play—' The tears came again; Helen tried to remove Fiona's arms, but she clung tightly to her and, to Helen's dismay, Fiona herself began to cry. 'Hush, Fiona dear, it's nothing, nothing at all.'

'It is – it is! You're sad – you wouldn't cry if you weren't sad!'

'I'm not sad, sweetheart. Now be a good girl and stop crying.' Helen dried her own eyes, then turned up Fiona's flushed little face and wiped the tears from her cheeks. 'There now, everything's all right.'

'Why were you crying?' A tiny sob shook Fiona's body and Helen drew her close and held her for a moment without speaking.

'I wasn't feeling too well,' she said at length.

'You're poorly?' Fiona looked up at her anxiously. She seemed ready to burst into tears again.

'Not now.' Helen was still distressed at upsetting the child, and hoped she could reassure her that there was nothing seriously wrong. 'I'm fine now, darling. Shall we go out into the garden? Come on, I'll push you on the swing.' To her relief Fiona managed to produce a smile, and within minutes she was her usual laughing self again as she begged Helen to push her higher.

To Helen's astonishment Leon's eyes kindled with anger when, on his arrival home much earlier than usual, she gave him his aunt's message.

'Does she think I've nothing else on my mind except her bungalow?' he rasped. 'She'll just have to wait; there are other more important matters to be attended to at present.'

Helen could only stare. Why this show of temper? And what did his words mean? Had something gone wrong between him and Paula? Or could it be that the affair was becoming too involved? She was forced to ask,

'What are these important matters, Leon?' But he shook his head, refusing to enlighten her, even as she expected he would.

He seemed utterly harassed, and there was a slight droop of dejection about his shoulders. She noticed his eyes, too. How tired they were. And those little tints of grey at his temples – they were almost white! What could be wrong? Something very serious, obviously, and for a brief space love and tenderness were her only emotions; she ached to put her arms around him, to press his head to her breast, and comfort him. But the next moment she hardened her heart. Whatever had gone amiss could only concern Paula Maxwell. And if he chose to indulge in an affair like that then he himself must shoulder any troubles or anxieties which might result from it. Why should she waste her pity on him? He had spared no pity for her.

He scarcely spoke a word to her for the next hour or two, and when Chippy came in and began throwing his ball in the air, and catching it, he snapped at him and told him to keep to the garden.

'Leon!' The exclamation came involuntarily to Helen's lips. 'There's no need to speak to Chippy like that.'

'Is it usual for him to play ball games in the house?'

'It couldn't exactly be called a ball game—'

'He's not playing in the house!'

Her eyes blazed.

'You have no need to shout,' she retorted. 'I'm not deaf.'

He glared at her and opened his mouth to speak, then changed his mind and lapsed once more into a brooding silence. Helen was fuming. For over a fortnight she had spent her evenings alone. For once he had come home early and all he could do was to vent his anger on her and the children. She went and joined them in the garden, leaving him alone in the sitting-room. But after a while he came and told her he was going to see his aunt.

'I'd better let her know how far I've progressed,' he said. His voice had lost its edge, but his ill-temper remained. Helen could sense it in his whole demeanour.

'You've made some progress, then? Have you found her a smaller place?'

'The very thing, but the price is higher than she is expecting to pay. However, her old house has fetched an excellent price, so she'll still be a good deal in pocket.' He pushed a hand wearily through his dark hair and turned away. He still seemed greatly troubled, and very tired.

His mood strangely affected Helen herself and, unable to face another evening alone, she kept the children with her and they were still up when, to her surprise, Leon returned just before nine o'clock.

'I kept them up for company,' she explained in answer to his inquiry. 'They can go to bed now, though.' They'd been bathed and were sitting on the rug in their dressing gowns, doing jig-saw puzzles. 'Put those away,' she said, and, with a glance of apology at Leon. 'I'll go and prepare their supper. They'll soon be in bed.'

'It doesn't matter. Leave them for a while.' He hesitated. 'Bring their supper in here.'

Leave them? Leon was always so firm about their bedtime.

Shrugging, she went into the kitchen and set out their supper on a tray. She had pulled the sitting-room door to behind her on leaving, but it had swung open and Helen stopped, the tray in her hand, taking in the intimate little scene being enacted there. Fiona was on her uncle's knee, one arm round his neck, her cheek resting against his. Chippy was still on the rug, putting away the jig-saw puzzles and looking far from happy. Leon glanced down and said,

'What's the matter, Chippy?'

Chippy shook his head dumbly and, resting his eyes on Fiona for a moment, he began to blink rapidly. He was ready to cry, Helen realized with a frown. The child returned his attention to the jig-saw puzzles, tossing the pieces in the box and sliding on the lid. Leon asked him again what was wrong.

'You don't love me as much as you love Fiona.' He pushed the box away from him and kept his eyes fixed upon it.

'What makes you say that?'

'You shouted at me – when I played with my ball. You were in a bad temper.'

'So I was.' Leon reached down a hand to the boy. 'I'm sorry, Chippy. Come and sit on my knee.'

Chippy glanced up in surprise, as well he might. Leon apologizing! Chippy did as he was told and both children sat there. Leon's face was hidden from her, but Helen could sense a deep unhappiness in him. If only he would tell her what was wrong! But he would scarcely do that, seeing that his troubles were concerned with Paula Maxwell.

'Do you love Chippy as much as me?' Fiona leant away and examined her uncle's dark face.

'I love you both equally.'

He spoke the truth, Helen knew. For although at first he hadn't been particularly enthusiastic about having them, there was no doubt that he had grown to love them dearly.

'That means as much as each other,' Chippy informed his sister knowledgeably. 'That's right, isn't it, Uncle Leon?'

'That's right, Chippy.'

Helen could only continue to stare. That tremulous note in Leon's voice, a note that seemed to break with sheer misery. And his arms . . . how tightly they held both Chippy and Fiona. It almost seemed that he would never let them go.

'What's the matter with me?' Helen chided herself, taking the tray into the room. She was always imagining things these days.

'Have you settled everything with Aunt Chrisoula?' She just had to say something, to ease the strain within her. 'Is she willing to have the bungalow you've found for her?'

Leon nodded. His glance in her direction was casual and she felt he had not really noticed her at all.

'She's happy about the whole deal.' He took his arm from about his nephew's waist and Chippy slid down on to the rug, looking up expectantly at the tray in Helen's hands. 'At least that's one small worry off my mind.'

One. . . .

When the children were in bed she washed up their supper dishes and put them away. What was the terrible problem on her husband's mind? Could it concern something other than his relationship with Paula? Could it be money?

When she returned to the sitting-room he was on the couch, his head sunk in his hands. Her heart seemed to be wrenched right out of her and she went swiftly to him, forgetting Paula, forgetting all the dissension, all the angry words that had passed between them – forgetting everything but the sure fact that she still loved him, that, whatever he had done to her in the past, whatever he did to her in the future, she would never cease to care.

'Leon. . . .' Timidly she touched his sleeve. 'Leon, can't you tell me what is wrong?' His head was slowly raised, but he stared at her unseeingly. 'What is it?' Her hand tightened round his arm. 'Is it money? Have you had a big loss, or something?'

'No, Helen, it is not money I have lost.'

The way he had said that. . . . The strange significance in his voice. He *had* lost something, that was plain.

'Then what—?' Why ask? Paula must have thrown him over. . . . Unconsciously Helen shook her head. Paula would never do that. 'Leon, can't you tell me what's wrong?'

He did not answer at once, but became lost in thought, and Helen gained the impression that he was endeavouring to make a decision. But when at last he did speak, it was merely to say, quietly but firmly,

'No, Helen, I can't tell you what is wrong.'

Withdrawing her hand, she turned slowly away, pain

176

and bitterness in her heart. For there was no mistaking the emphasis on the word 'you'. And that could mean only one thing. His unhappiness *was* concerned with Paula, for had it stemmed from any other cause there was no reason why he should not tell her about it.

They had to be up early on the Friday, for Leon wanted to join the convoy. This meant that they would be in Nicosia before eight o'clock and Helen said they had better stay at the office for a while as she could not turn up at Trudy's at this time of the morning, especially as she had the children with her.

'I'm afraid I shall be busy,' Leon said, and Helen sensed an awkwardness about him as he went on, 'I'll drive you straight to the flat. I'm sure Trudy won't mind. She's bound to be up, for she knows you're coming fairly early – she must do because I said you'd all come down with me.'

'But eight o'clock. . . . No, Leon. If you don't want us at the office we'll walk round for a little while.'

'It isn't that I don't want you, but I'll be busy.' No sign of apology in his voice. But it was clear why he did not want her at the office. He need not have worried, though, she would never ask about her painting. She had too much pride for that.

'Don't worry, Leon,' she said stiffly. 'We can go and have some coffee.'

'But I want to go to the office,' Fiona put in. 'I've only seen it once.'

'We'll sit quietly,' Chippy said persuasively. 'Let us come to the office, Uncle Leon.'

'Very well.' Although he sounded faintly impatient, there was resignation in his voice also, as if the effort of argument were just too much trouble for him.

Theo was already there when they arrived at the lovely white building that served as Leon's office. He was outside, watering the numerous flowering plants that grew in pots all along the walls and on the sides of the steps. The colours made a brilliant contrast to the dazzling whiteness of the building and again Helen thought it looked more like a beautiful modern villa than an office.

'It's lovely!' Fiona walked about on the thick carpet, gazing all around her. 'It wasn't like this before.'

'It was exactly like this before,' her uncle assured her, adding, 'But you didn't notice it — for you felt rather strange, I expect.' Strange and anxious, yes, recollected Helen. For hadn't they both said their uncle was horrid? And she herself had been so perturbed, wondering how they would fare with a man who was known to have a dislike for children. But in no time at all he had grown to love them, and they had soon returned their love. If only Leon could care for her, she thought, what a happy family they would be.

They were in the outer office, the one used by Theo. Leon was about to go through to his own office when the phone rang. He picked up the receiver and instantly his expression became guarded. A swift glance in Helen's direction left her in no doubt that he would prefer her to be anywhere but here. His words were also guarded and presently he put a hand over the receiver and spoke to her.

'Do you mind taking the children out, Helen? I'm sorry, but this call is private. You can go into my office.'

Her face paled, but she made no answer as, with a gentle push, she sent the children before her into Leon's office.

'What shall we do?' Chippy became restless within minutes and began flicking the papers on the desk.

'Just sit down and be quiet. When Uncle Leon's finished his phoning we'll tell him we're going. We can have some refreshments at a café and then it will be time to go to Auntie Trudy's.'

Chippy obeyed, choosing Leon's chair and, no doubt, feeling rather important sitting there at his uncle's desk.

Who could be on the other end of that phone? It was a woman, for Helen had heard her voice; a woman who obviously knew of Leon's intention of arriving early at the office. What had been said to cause that guarded expression to enter Leon's eyes? All Helen had been allowed to hear was,

'I made it out yesterday, but when you phoned and said it wasn't enough I naturally held it back – you said you'd phone again this morning – yes, certainly you can have it. . . .'

Helen stood by the desk, but her eyes were on Theo, who was now watering the plants on the verandah. Then he disappeared in response to a call from Leon and a moment or two later he had entered the office and as he walked towards the desk some papers, and Leon's cheque book, fell to the floor.

'Chippy, you shouldn't touch.' Bending down, Helen made to pick them up, but Theo was before her.

'This is what Mr. Petrou wants.' He held up the cheque book, obviously feeling some explanation was necessary. 'The cheque for the lady. I take it to her.' He grinned and then, extracting a cheque, he placed the book in a drawer, out of Chippy's way. He went out; Helen heard him call, 'I'll be back in twenty minutes, Mr. Petrou,' and then she heard his van start up and a moment later it flashed past the office window.

The lady. . . . Helen's blue eyes flickered and darkened. The cheque book had come open as it fell; she had seen the amount, but not the name. Five million *mils* . . . five thousand pounds! And the lady of whom Theo spoke could not be far away, for he had said he would be back in twenty minutes. Her gaze moved to the drawer in which the cheque book lay, and then to Chippy sitting there, on her husband's chair. Fiona had wandered out on to the verandah. The idea of what she contemplated doing caused her heartbeats to quicken painfully. It was wrong – but she had to know. For it might not be Paula– Oh, please don't let it be Paula, she prayed silently.

'Chippy, why don't you go out to Fiona?' The voice did not sound like hers, it was so high-pitched and cracked. Although Chippy at once obliged, Helen found herself unable to move. But she could not take her eyes off the drawer. . . .

The date, and 'P', that was all – except for the amount. Tremblingly Helen returned the cheque book and closed the drawer. So her stupid little prayer had been all in vain – as she had known it would be.

For what purpose had he given her the money? Had Paula got herself into debt? That seemed the only feasible explanation; that was why Leon was so plainly anxious and distressed. She looked up as he entered the office. Yes, much of the anxiety had now left his face, though he still seemed faintly troubled. But that was only to be expected, for one did not part with a sum like that without having some regrets.

'We're going now,' she began, when Fiona ran in and interrupted her.

'Uncle Leon, I don't feel well!' She clung to him and started to cry. 'It's awful!'

'Where does it hurt?' Leon picked her up and sat her on his knee. 'Is it your tummy?'

She shook her head.

'No, I don't know what it is. It's gone now.'

'Well, that was quick.' He looked quizzically at her. 'And tears. . . .' He took his handkerchief and dried her eyes. 'Big girls don't cry just because they don't feel well.'

'Aunt Helen's a big girl, and she cries when she's not well.'

'Does she?' His eyes sought Helen's; she blushed and glanced away. 'When was Aunt Helen ill?'

'The other day – and she cried a lot, didn't you, Aunt Helen?' Chippy called to her then and, without waiting for an answer, Fiona slid off her uncle's knee and went out, obviously cured.

'Why were you crying, Helen?' No longer was her husband's voice soft and gentle; on the contrary, the sudden harshness in it startled her.

'As Fiona said, I didn't feel well.'

'Don't lie, there's no need. You must have been more than a little upset to have allowed Fiona to see you in tears. I presume it was on account of my not allowing you to see your English friend?'

She stared at him in bewilderment.

'I don't think I understand you, Leon?'

'What else is there you could cry about?'

'I still don't understand you. Why should you bring him up? It isn't as if we've been very friendly—'

'Friendly! That's a mild word. You're more than friends, much more, so you needn't stand there trying to fool me!'

Her bewilderment grew. Why the outburst – and at this particular time?

'How dare you say that? I scarcely know him!' What right had he to sit there hurling out accusations when he had just given Paula Maxwell five thousand pounds? Should she tell him she knew all about it? But no, for he had a right to do what he liked with his money, and he would not hesitate to tell her so.

'You know him well enough to have him at my house—'

'At—? How do you know?

'I was told. These things have a way of getting around.'

'But who—' Her face flamed with anger as comprehension dawned. 'She told you!'

'She?'

181

'You know very well. Paula Maxwell!'

'Correct, she did.'

'But—' Helen stared at him in bewilderment. He had known all the time, and yet not mentioned it until now. It was not like Leon to remain quiet about a thing like that. Why hadn't he seized the opportunity of subjecting her once again to a violent scene? To know that Robert had actually been in his house, and fail even to mention it . . . it was scarcely credible 'Why didn't you say something about it before now?'

'I had my reasons.'

'What reasons?' Helen asked, puzzled.

'They're not important now. What is important is that I'm not having my wife running around with men from the village—'

'Men!' she flashed. 'Oh, you shall not say that to me! How can you when you're running around with *her*!'

'Her?' He looked amazed and Helen's fury increased. She flung at him everything she knew. 'Paula Maxwell! She told you about Robert, did she? Well, I'll tell you something. When Robert answered that phone she thought it was you, and was talking about the picnic you'd both arranged—'

'Picnic?' He sat up in his chair, a look of utter amazement on his face. His manner only served to increase her fury and she went on quiveringly,

'Yes, a picnic – and you needn't look like that, you know all about it! She was telling you to bring food and drinks – because you were going off into the wilds somewhere.' The last sentence came slowly and deliberately, so that every word could sink in. But then she paused, bewildered, for her husband was now leaning back in his chair, his hands thrust in his pockets . . . and the look on his face was actually a mixture of amusement and relief! And to add to her bewilderment his voice was infuriatingly calm as he said, very softly,

'Helen, you really believe this? Is it the reason for – for—? Is this what's been troubling you?'

'Believe it? Of course I do. Everyone knows about you and Paula – Robert told me you were going about with her before you met me. Are you trying to deny it?'

'Paula and I were friends once, but—'

'You still are! And as for its troubling me, you flatter yourself. I don't care if you g-go out with a – a dozen w-women! I don't care that you're with her every evening, or that you gave her my painting – when you'd said you liked it so much—' To her dismay hot tears filled her eyes, but she managed to suppress them as she continued wildly, no longer holding anything back. 'I don't care that you've given her five thousand pounds—'

'You—! How do you know that?'

She explained what had happened, adding defiantly, 'Robert is my friend and I don't care what you think of me. I d-don't care about – about anything—' Turning, she ran from the office, endeavouring to calm herself as she called to the children. She heard her husband's voice urgently calling her back but she ran on, almost colliding with a tall, grey-haired gentleman who was just entering the building. She heard Leon's voice again, coming closer.

'Helen, you silly little—'

'Leon, a very good morning to you. About that plot of land you were advising me to buy. . . .'

# CHAPTER TEN

IT was only to be expected that Trudy would notice something was amiss, and when, soon after their arrival, the children went down to explore the grounds, she turned anxiously to Helen and asked her what was wrong.

'It's nothing, Trudy,' she quivered. The tears were very close; she must not cry, though. At all costs she must hide her unhappiness. But Trudy was not to be put off, and before Helen knew it she was pouring out the whole story to her friend. Trudy was horrified, staring at her in disbelief at first, but gradually accepting the truth of Helen's story.

'He gave her five thousand pounds?'

'So you see, he must be madly in love with her.'

'Then why didn't he marry her? He knew her before he knew you, so you've just said?'

'She always expected to marry him, but he wasn't the marrying sort – and he probably wouldn't ever have married if it hadn't been for the sake of the children.'

'Five thousand pounds. . . .' Trudy whistled. 'She's got him where she wants him, there's no doubt of that.' She gave her friend a flickering glance. 'And you hit back by saying you had a boy-friend' She paused again, thinking about this for a time, and then, 'That wouldn't help the situation at all.'

'Nothing can worsen the situation between us – oh, if only I could leave him, but I can't Trudy. I shall never leave Chippy and Fiona.'

'They'll bring you happiness, Helen, I'm sure of that.' She put an arm around Helen's shoulders and her own voice broke slightly as she said, 'That this should happen to you, of all people! As if once wasn't enough – it seems impossible that it could happen again.'

'It has, nevertheless, and it's my own fault, Trudy. I swore never to care for anyone again, never to let another man hurt me. It's my own fault,' she repeated, tears trickling down her face.

'What I can't understand is why he told you all this about Robert only this morning. He must have known for some time.'

'He has, and I'm puzzled by it too, because, come to think of it, he's been most cautious lately.' Her eyes opened very wide as she stared at her friend wonderingly. 'Why should he be cautious?'

'I don't know what you mean.'

Helen could not explain. But looking back now she was convinced that Leon had most certainly been practising caution these past few weeks. He'd been cool with her, yes, but there had been no scenes, no sharp words even. And he had kept away. . . . She had reasoned that this was because his desire had waned, but now she was not so sure. Could it be that, for some reason, he had not wanted to upset her? – or cause her to be too dissatisfied with her life? This conviction grew even though she saw no explanation for it. But why the sudden change? Had she not retaliated this morning he would once again have subjected her to a violent scene, once more have made her feel the power of his domination.

Again she asked herself why the change and still she found no answer.

'There's something I don't understand, Trudy,' she said, speaking her thoughts aloud. 'But it doesn't matter, because it can't possibly make any difference to Leon and me.'

'I'm still very puzzled by the whole thing,' Trudy said later when they were having lunch. 'Leon doesn't strike me at all as a man who would deliberately hurt you like

185

this. Tasos has a great admiration for him.'

A bitter curve touched Helen's lips. Hurt? That was a mild word to use for Leon's treatment of her on occasions. But there had been those other times. . . . Her eyes clouded as memories came flooding back to her. They *had* been happy, and it had seemed that Leon wanted nothing more than to be with her and the children. She recalled her own feelings for her husband, developing so slowly, and against her will. But she had given up the struggle, and let him have all her love. They had come so close and she had known a happiness she would never have believed possible. And then the discovery that Leon had given her painting to Paula Maxwell. That had been the beginning of it all. . . .

'Aunt Helen, can we go for a walk after lunch?' Chippy's voice broke into her thoughts as she glanced up to smile at him.

'Is it all right with you?' she asked her friend.

'Quite. I love walking.'

And so they went out, eventually ending up in the park. They stopped for refreshments, sitting out in a lovely garden with a roof of vines to shelter them from the blistering heat of the sun.

'We've been out a long while,' said Fiona, beginning to flag. 'Oh, I'm so tired!'

It was four o'clock when they arrived back at the flat and Leon was outside, sitting in the car. Helen's heart missed a beat, but she managed to keep her voice steady as she said,

'You're early, Leon.' He had come from the car and was standing beside it, eyeing her with a most odd expression.

'I've been waiting for over two hours.'

'Have you? All that time, Uncle Leon?' Fiona took his hand and held it to her cheek. 'We've been walking for miles and miles!'

'Have you come to take us home?' Chippy wanted to know. Leon nodded and Chippy went on, 'Aunt Helen said we were going home on the bus.'

'What Aunt Helen says and what I say are two different things,' Leon murmured, still regarding her with that odd expression. 'She has the most peculiar notions at times, Chippy, the most peculiar notions.' No mistaking the deeper significance of those words. Helen stared at him, conscious of Trudy's interest and feeling embarrassed by it.

'Shall we go in?' Trudy said at last, leading the way to the stairs. 'I'm dying with thirst, I don't know how the rest of you feel.' She immediately went into the kitchen to make the drinks. The others went into the sitting-room.

'You two,' Leon said, 'off you go and play.'

'Play?' Fiona protested, flopping into a chair. 'I'm tired!'

'So am I.' Chippy found another chair and sat down.

'They – really are tired,' Helen hastily submitted as a sternness touched Leon's lips. She vividly recalled her conduct of the morning and a sudden trembling seized her. She had no wish to be alone with her husband.

'Who told you I gave your picture away?' he asked, allowing the children to stay.

'The hairdresser from the village.' Her voice sounded stilted and far too high-pitched. 'I couldn't believe it,' she added, her lip quivering.

'I should have thought you were above taking notice of village gossip,' he said with a hint of reproach. 'You really believed I would part with it after saying I wanted it for my office?'

Helen swallowed. There was something wrong, for although the censure remained in Leon's eyes there was an unmistakable light of tenderness in them too.

'It isn't in your office.'

'I must correct you, my dear. It is in my office.'

'But – but it wasn't. . . .' She took a little step towards him. 'If you didn't give it to her, where has it been? I thought you gave it to her because – because –' She broke off, aware that both children were listening interestedly to what she was saying.

'The explanation's very simple, my dear,' he said, ignoring her last words. 'And if only you had asked me when you first heard about it we'd both have been saved a good deal of unhappiness.' He went on to tell her that the man interested in buying the old mill had been sent to him originally by Paula. On seeing the painting in his office he had wanted to buy it, but Leon had naturally refused to sell. 'He then asked if I'd let you do another, for him. But I'm selfish; I want to have the only one done by my wife. However, I did lend it to him to have a copy made. Paula knew an artist who would do this, and that is how she came to have your painting. I now have it back and it has a place of honour in my office.' He shook his head a little sadly. 'How could you believe that of me, Helen?'

'I don't know.' She twisted her hands distractedly. 'It wasn't in your office when I was there the day before, and when Eleni said Paula had it I naturally concluded that you'd given it to her.' She looked up at him, her gaze still uncertain. 'You have an explanation for that,' she whispered, 'but all the other things. . . .' She stopped, shaking her head. What excuse could there be for giving Paula five thousand pounds? But could it be that he had merely lent it to her? Unaware of the light of hope that shone in her eyes, she added impulsively, 'Have you an explanation for those?

'I have an explanation for everything,' he replied blandly.

'Everything . . . ?' She looked up at him with a wide and questioning gaze. 'Everything, Leon?'

'You're a little idiot, Helen,' he murmured in tones of tender humour. 'What must I do with you?'

'Leon, what is the explanation?' Helen looked at him beseechingly. 'I've been so miserable.'

Leon did not speak for a while; his eyes strayed over to where Fiona was sitting, swinging her legs and listening intently to all that was being said. Chippy was equally interested and at last Leon said firmly,

'Come, you two, off to the car.'

'Are you taking us home, Uncle Leon?' Fiona slid from the chair and tilted her head to look up at him. A most odd expression entered his eyes as he said softly,

'Yes, Fiona, I'm taking you home. Chippy, go and get in the car.' He watched them leave and then, 'Come, my love, it's time we were on our way.'

'But, Leon, you said you'd explain?'

'Not here, sweetheart.' He smiled tenderly down at her. 'When we get home – and the children are in bed.'

'I can't stand it!' exclaimed Trudy a moment later when they made their apologies for leaving so suddenly. 'Leon, what's happening? You can't just go off like this and leave me high and dry!'

'High and dry?' he echoed absently, his tender gaze still on Helen's face.

'Helen was terribly upset when she arrived here—'

'Trudy, no—' Helen flushed vividly and tried to stop her.

'And now you're rushing off without telling me a thing. Leon, have pity on a woman's curiosity!'

'We're going home to sort out a few little mis-understandings,' he obliged, adding, 'And that dinner – you can send us your invitation whenever you like. We're at liberty any evening.'

Trudy glanced from one to the other and gave a satisfied little smile.

'I will,' she said. 'And we'll make it a celebration.'

For a long while the only sound in the car was that of the children's chatter, and then Helen spoke.

'You left the office early.' It was merely for something to say and her words were stiff and cold. Leon did not appear to notice.

'I'd have left much earlier, but I had some very important business to see to.'

Another silence and then, timidly,

'Leon, you said you could explain.'

'What I have to say can't be said before Chippy and Fiona.' A sudden harshness entered his voice and Helen turned her head in surprise. The line of his jaw was hard and his mouth compressed. She sank back in her seat and asked him no further questions.

They were out on the verandah when he told her what he had been through since the day the children's mother appeared and threatened to take them from him.

'I saw immediately that she had no real interest in them,' he went on. 'It was money she wanted. I suppose I gave myself away, let her see how much Chippy and Fiona meant to me, and so she kept on haggling over the sum – changing her mind and wanting more. However, she decided to settle for five thousand – though I'd have gone higher had she persisted.' They were standing against the rail and as Leon stopped speaking the only sound for a while was the faint whisper of the breeze in the palms fringing the garden. Then Helen said in a frightened little voice,

'She can't take them, Leon, not now?'

He shook his head firmly.

'That was my chief anxiety, but I refused to let her have any money at all unless she agreed to a legal adoption. We have been settling this today – that's what kept me so long. No, darling, no one is ever going to take them from us.' He drew her close and once again she felt his great tenderness, and his strength.

'If only you'd let me share your troubles—' Helen broke off guiltily and added with sincere regret, 'I've been such a fool, Leon. I don't know how you can forgive me.'

'You forgave me once, remember?' and when she did not reply, 'It was never as you thought, darling. It was always because I loved you.' He held her away and looked anxiously down at her. 'You do believe that, Helen? You must!'

'I do – oh, Leon, why didn't I know then?'

'It was because of that other hurt. You believed all men were the same; it was only natural.' He bent to kiss her and it was a long while before he said, on a note of tender humour, 'There's just one other minor point, my silly little love. You accused me of going off on picnics with Paula. She sells small properties, as you know, and I had her looking round for something for Aunt Chrisoula. She had a whole list and I can assure you, my love, that it was no picnic for me to run around searching for one at the price my aunt wanted to pay.'

Helen was silent, her fair head bent. After a little while he put a finger under her chin and she was forced to meet his gaze.

'I don't know how you can forgive me,' she said again, her voice low and husky. 'I – I just kept on jumping to conclusions.'

'Well, for that matter, so did I,' he admitted. 'But I was so damned jealous of your Englishman—'

'He's not my Englishman – and you'd no need in the least to be jealous.'

'You'd been out swimming with him, and I was mad with—'

'Swimming? How do you know that?'

'You left your beach bag in the porch, and Fiona, as you know, cannot help poking into everything.' He paused and Helen almost flinched as his grip tightened on her arm. 'I saw red when she brought out that wet costume. I knew it must be Robert because you didn't know anyone else.'

She thought about this for a moment, and then, on a puzzled note,

'Leon, why didn't you tell me about it at the time? I mean, you only mentioned it this morning.'

'I admit I wanted to tackle you about spending that afternoon with him, but I dared not.' He actually shuddered and her arms tightened lovingly. 'You see, darling, I knew that should Mrs. Petrou take the children, you would be free to leave me, because it was only the children that kept you here—'

'No – no, it wasn't, Leon,' she assured him hastily. 'I would never have left you, darling, so you needn't have worried.'

'But I believed you would, and I was so very cautious, not daring to antagonize you or make you dissatisfied with your life. For I was so afraid of losing you.' He drew her close and she felt the tender strength of his lips on hers.

The breeze brought the scent of the pines drifting down from the hillside. All was silent, and she whispered huskily,

'You'll never lose me, Leon, I'm yours for ever.'